FIGHT FOR FREEDOM

Eleanor Watkins

CHRISTIAN FOCUS PUBLICATIONS

© 1993 Eleanor Watkins
ISBN 1 85792 033 3

Published by
Christian Focus Publications Ltd
Geanies House, Fearn, Ross-shire,
IV20 1TW, Scotland, Great Britain.

Cover design by Donna Macleod
Cover illustration by Shona Grant

Printed and bound in Great Britain by
Cox & Wyman Ltd, Reading, Berkshire

CONTENTS

CHAPTER 1 7
CHAPTER 2 14
CHAPTER 3. 20
CHAPTER 4 27
CHAPTER 5 33
CHAPTER 6 38
CHAPTER 7 46
CHAPTER 8 53
CHAPTER 9 59
CHAPTER 10 67
CHAPTER 11 73
CHAPTER 12 81
CHAPTER 13 86
CHAPTER 14 91
CHAPTER 15 99
CHAPTER 16 106
CHAPTER 17 113
CHAPTER 18 119
CHAPTER 19 125
CHAPTER 20 133
CHAPTER 21 140
CHAPTER 22 146

Chapter 1

The late afternoon sun sent its rays slantwise through thick spreading branches, dappling the leaf mould in patches and causing the lonely boy rider to squeeze his tired eyes tight against the brightness. His dark hair hung in damp tangles about his thin face, and his shoulders drooped as he sat slumped in the sheepskin saddle, holding the reins loosely and feeling the itch of stale perspiration drying on the skin of his back. The horse's ears drooped in weariness too, its head hanging a little and its hooves muffled by thick leaf mould as it plodded between the trees.

It had been a long day for them both. They had hunted since sunrise, the pony and the boy, setting out early that morning with high hopes of a day's freedom from dull routine, and possibly fresh meat and game to vary the usual winter diet of dried mutton and venison. Caradoc had hunted alone, for his brother Owain's pony - the best in the village - was lame, and Owain would not ride one of the lesser ones. Their father had warned Caradoc not to wander too far in his hunting, for a twelve-year-old boy far from home would make an easy target for an arrow or spear from some member of a neighbouring tribe. Caradoc had agreed in high spirits, certain that he would soon come across a wild pig to spear and carry home in triumph. But he had seen no pig at all, nor even a deer close enough to aim at. The only results of the day's hunting were slung across the pony's shoulders in front of him - a pigeon or two and a large hare, rather tough and stringy at this time of year. Those expecting pork or venison would be disappointed.

But he had enjoyed the day, and none the less for having spent it alone. It was not often that he had time to himself, and he made the most of the moments when they came. At noon he and the pony had stopped by a little woodland spring where he had sat among the ferns and eaten the lunch packed by his grandmother, while the pony grazed. Now noon seemed far in the past and he was hungry again, his stomach growling with emptiness and his throat dry.

The pony stumbled a little and Caradoc reined it to a halt. Another clear little stream sparkled ahead of him, and he dismounted stiffly and knelt to drink from cupped hands. The pony drank too, then began to crop at the fresh green grass and dandelion sprouting by the water. Caradoc rested for a moment, his arm over the pony's shoulders, noticing the soft woodland sounds of early spring. A twittering of building birds in the branches above him, the gentle cooing of wood pigeons a little further away. A soft haze of new green was spreading over the limp brown undergrowth, powdery yellow lambs' tails swung from the hazels, and beech trees were unfurling their tender green leaves. Soon the sound of the cuckoo would herald another new season, and the days would be full of light and warmth. Caradoc heaved a sigh, wondering again about the world outside the forest, vast and open and mysterious, with its wide spaces and mountains and rivers and its unknown people. This outside land filled him with curiosity, and he longed to know more of it. But Owain only laughed when he talked of these things, and no-one else seemed able to give proper answers to his questions.

He sighed again, and then gave a huge yawn. The afternoon was drawing in, and they were still a long way from home. He climbed into the saddle, and the pony, though refreshed by food and drink, was still eager for home and stable and set off at a brisk walk.

For a while they climbed, then the ground levelled out for a space, the trees thinned, and the boy's knees urged the pony to a faster pace. They were re-entering the trees at the far end of the clearing when a sudden rustle sounded from the undergrowth almost under their feet. Reining in his mount, Caradoc found himself staring down into the small red eyes and curved yellow tusks of a wild boar disturbed from rest.

Caradoc's tiredness fell away. For a moment he stared into the small piggy eyes in the hairy face, noticing the cruel tusks that could rend and tear the flesh of a man to shreds. Boar had been known to attack a mounted man, and as this one snarled, Caradoc's pony flung up its head in fear. Then with a crashing and snorting the wild pig had turned and was rushing away on short powerful legs.

Caradoc's heart thumped. Maybe there would be roast pig for supper after all! He urged the tired horse forward with a flailing of knees and heels, reaching for his spear. The boar was tearing through the undergrowth with a great crashing and snorting, leaving a clear trail. With a magnificent effort the pony surged forward, the gap closed, and Caradoc raised his spear arm high.

The next moment he found himself on the ground with all the breath knocked out of him and his head reeling. So intent upon the chase had he been, that he had not noticed the low branch of a beech tree which had caught his chest and knocked him sideways from the saddle. Somewhere ahead of him the boar crashed away into the distance, while behind him the frightened horse snorted, tossed its head and shied sideways away from its fallen rider.

When Caradoc had recovered his wind a little, he sat up and tried to rise, but a searing pain shot through his ankle. He groaned and sank back against the trunk of the beech tree that had felled him. The pony, with a great lack of loyalty, had disappeared without a backward look. No doubt, the boy reasoned, it would turn up at the village and a search would be mounted. Trying to ignore the pain which shot through his leg whenever he moved, he settled himself as comfortably as he could for a long wait.

Night was approaching fast and the air was chill with a hint of frost. Somewhere close at hand an owl screeched and another answered further in the wood. There was the sharp yip of a vixen, and a scurry of short legs - a hedgehog maybe. The small night creatures were coming to life. Somewhere far away a wolf howled, and there was a distant crashing that might be the same wild boar returning. Caradoc shivered a little, and thought longingly of his own hut, with a bright fire and Islean stirring a savoury stew over it. He did not relish the thought of a night alone in the forest. But his leg would not bear his weight and there was nothing else to do. In spite of cold and hunger, pain and helplessness, he dozed a little, his head lolling against the beech trunk. He was awakened with a start by the sound of another human voice. At first he thought it was his father come for him, and started up eagerly to greet him. But he saw at once through the remaining dim light that the man was a stranger.

Caradoc drew back and gathered himself tensely against the beech trunk, like some wounded young animal at bay. His heart beat hard against his ribs. The stranger was strange indeed, to Caradoc's eyes - a large man in a shapeless garment of some rough cloth, and no weapon that Caradoc could see. He had dismounted from a donkey, which scarcely seemed large enough to bear his weight, and was bending forward to peer into the face of the injured boy.

He held out a hand to Caradoc, saying something in a strange tongue. Caradoc struck at the hand and spat out the words "Keep away!"

The large man withdrew his hand and smiled. "Ah! A young Celtic eagle fallen from its eyrie, I see!" And then, to Caradoc's surprise, he said in the boy's own tongue "Where are you hurt?"

Caradoc did not reply, staring fiercely at the man through the gathering twilight. When the man came nearer, he tried to pull himself to his feet, but the pain shot sharply upward and he sank down again. Then he

11

remembered the sharp skinning knife in his belt and reached behind him for it. But the man was quicker still, seizing the arm and applying pressure until the knife fell.

"I'll take that, my young savage! I see it is your ankle that is damaged. You must let me help you unless you want to take your chances with the wild beasts overnight! Will you come with me?"

In answer, Caradoc struck out again, and said from between clenched teeth, spitting out the words "I will not!"

"Very well, since you won't do it the easy way we must try the difficult," said the stranger resignedly. He made a sudden dart for the boy, moving surprisingly lightly for one of his girth, and seized him in a strong grip that pinioned Caradoc's arms to his sides. Caradoc shrieked with rage and pain, kicked with his good foot and tried to sink his teeth into the man's brawny arm. But he was no match for the stranger. In a short space of time he found himself helpless, his hands bound behind him with the girdle the man wore at his waist.

"Now!" said the stranger, panting a little. "On to the donkey, I think, and home, where I can properly attend to that ankle. If you would go quietly you would cause yourself far less pain."

Suddenly Caradoc felt all the fight drain out of him. He was desperately tired and in great pain. He knew he had no choice but to go with the man. He also knew that he would be killed, sooner or later. He did not believe a word that the man had said about helping him. Strangers always killed other strangers, swiftly or slowly, that was one of the rules of life. He would not die without a struggle, though. He'd bide his time and take the first chance he got to strike back.

But for the time being, he allowed himself to be loaded painfully onto the donkey's back and carted away like a load of birch faggots or a carcase of mutton.

Chapter 2

Caradoc afterwards remembered little of the journey, except that it seemed to go on for a very long time, and that it was bumpy, painful, weary and bone-shaking. He had resolved to stay alert, but in spite of himself his eyes kept closing and his head nodding. Time after time he jerked himself awake to strain his eyes through the darkness towards the sharp pricked ears of the donkey and the dark shapeless bulk of the man who led it. If Caradoc's hands had been free, he felt he would certainly have found a weapon - a stick or an odd stone left in his pouch - that he would have used to attack the stranger. His spear and bow, slung across the pony's back, had probably fallen off and been lost in the woods along with the game; they had been only loosely fastened. He ground his teeth in helpless rage, thinking of the loss of the good weapons and of his own predicament. But there was nothing else he could do. He had to be content with glaring murderously at the broad back of the man in front.

A half-moon had risen and he was soon able to see

that they had left behind the thickly-wooded slopes of his home and emerged into flatter, more open country. They had plodded for a long time under the moon when the low dark bulk of some rough building, with smaller buildings huddled around it, all surrounded by a fence, loomed ahead. The tired donkey seemed to brighten, its ears pricked and its step quickened. Caradoc had the feeling that the donkey disliked carrying him as much as he disliked riding it, and would be mightily glad to shed its load. Before they reached the fence a door in it was flung open, and a figure emerged holding high a smoking torch.

"John - it is you! God be praised! We had all but given you up for lost!"

"Yes, it is I - and a guest. Take the donkey, Alwyn, and then come and help!"

They spoke in Caradoc's own tongue, though with a slightly different accent, and relief and gladness were in their voices. He found himself bundled from the back of the donkey and half-carried into a room where the man called Alwyn placed the torch into a bracket on the wall. There Caradoc was dumped upon a low stool, blinking in the light and biting his lip to keep from crying out at the renewed pain.

The other man, smaller and younger than Caradoc's rescuer and clad in a similar garment of rough home-spun, returned and stood looking down at the boy, his eyes twinkling quizzically in the flickering light. "Well, Brother John, I thought it was a stray goat you had set out to search for!"

The other smiled, then stifled a huge yawn. "True. I fear I failed to find the speckled nanny - she has finally eluded us, I think - but I discovered this wild young mountain goat instead, strayed from its den among the rocks. Or maybe it's an eaglet from some high eyrie or a wolf cub from a mountain lair! At any rate, it has teeth and claws and knows well how to use them!"

He turned back his sleeve to show a long scratch where Caradoc's fingernails had drawn blood. Caradoc, his eyes darting fiercely from one to the other, were aware that the men were gently mocking him. To his own great humiliation, a tear of pain and outrage escaped from one eye and trickled down his cheek.

Immediately the face of the older man softened. "Come, let us not mock. He is hurt, and he is only a boy, not much more than twelve summers as far as I can judge. Let us see to his ankle. Bring bandages and healing salve."

Caradoc felt himself helpless in their hands. Dumbly he gritted his teeth and bore the pain while they worked over his injured ankle, drawing off the deerskin leggings and boots and showing the swollen and discoloured flesh. The man called John moved the ankle gently back and forth.

"Not broken, I think, but badly wrenched. We'll soon have it right."

They bathed the ankle, applied a soothing ointment and bound it tightly with strips of cloth, which eased the throbbing almost at once.

"Now," said the man called John, straightening up and rubbing his back as though it ached. "A night's sleep, and I think it will be much improved."

Caradoc stared at him without speaking. He did not want to stay in this place with these strange people. The thought of it filled him with a kind of panic. But it was night, he was far from his own village home, and he was bone weary. When he was helped to a pallet nearby and covered with a rough warm blanket, he fell asleep almost at once.

It was broad daylight when he awoke, and the sun was streaming in through small window openings. There was none of the morning clamour that greeted each new day in Caradoc's mountain village, the barking and bleating of animals, stamp of horses' hooves, clank of weapons and shouting of human voices. A subdued hum of activity filled the place none the less, an impression of controlled routine and purpose. Presently a young man not very much older than Caradoc's brother Owain came in with a bowl of porridge, and goats' milk in a drinking vessel. The youth smiled at Caradoc but did not speak.

He placed the food on a low table of rough wood beside the boy and departed. Caradoc had instinctively drawn as far away as he could on his pallet, but he was ravenously hungry and thirsty. The food and drink might well be poisoned, he knew. Yet he took it and gobbled it to the last speck and drop. His rescuer, the elderly man called John, came a little later and looked at the ankle, unwinding the strips of linen and seeming pleased at the way the salve had done its work. Already the swelling was subsiding and the bruising fading. When helped to his feet, Caradoc found that he could stand and even hobble a little.

"Much better," said the big man with satisfaction, re-binding the ankle firmly. "Now, what are we to do with you? I suppose a wild eaglet like you wants to return to its eyrie, even though its wings are clipped?"

Caradoc sensed that the man was gently teasing again. He stared mutely for a moment, and then said hoarsely "I want to go home."

"Well then, so you shall. I'll take you part of the way on the old donkey, but I don't think I'll deliver you right to the door. I doubt that your people have any love for the likes of me. I daresay your ankle will hold out to carry you the rest of the way. I'll cut you a stout ash sapling to lean on. Rest there while I make ready."

He hurried off to some region beyond, and Caradoc was left alone. His first instinct was to dash for the door and escape, but a couple of steps told him that he would not get far alone, for his ankle was still weak, stiff and painful. He would have to wait for the man and the donkey. Setting his teeth, he sat down and gazed about at the many strange things that were in this place, his keen dark eyes missing nothing. The building was roughly constructed of wood and a simple wood table stood at one end of the room, with objects upon it, all strange to Caradoc. Across the open doorway one of the men passed, his shapeless garment hitched up to his knees and a hoe over his shoulder. A smell of cooking food came from somewhere close at hand.

Strangest of all was a carved picture fastened to the wall near the doorway. He stared at it for a long time. It was hewn from a flat piece of oak, the likeness of a man who seemed to be fastened to a wooden cross by his feet and his outstretched arms. Caradoc knew that the man was dying, but the expression on the suffering face was one of such sweetness that suddenly he was reminded of his own mother, though she had died before he could walk and he had no real memories of her. He wondered who the dying man could be.

Then John was back, and Caradoc was taken outside to where the same donkey waited in the sunshine, looking no happier than before. Climbing on its back, Caradoc saw vaguely a sweep of green valley with cultivated land near to the buildings, little plots of land where green spikes showed against the brown soil and the man with the tucked-up garment was bending over his hoe. John greeted him cheerfully and the other man waved his hoe at them.

"Our crops are doing well," said John with a touch of pride, taking the donkey's bridle. "We have planted barley, too, and hope for a good harvest this year."

Caradoc stared at him blankly. Crops - harvest - these were words he did not understand even in his own tongue. His people hunted and fought, what little food they grew was tended by the women. He felt scornful of this strange band of men who cooked and bandaged and did the work of women. He had realized by now that they were not going to kill him either, but just meekly send him on his way. They weren't really men at all, and how he and Owain and the others would laugh when he told them the tale.

Yet somehow a kind of grudging respect was mixed with the scorn. And strangely enough, his last thought as they headed for the wooded slope where his home perched high, was of the likeness of the dying man with the outstretched arms and sweet suffering face.

Chapter 3

The place where Caradoc's people had their home was a kind of plateau, half way up one of the thickly wooded mountain slopes forming part of the vast mountain ranges of the Welsh borders. The village perched there in a huddle of huts and animal shelters like the eyrie of some giant bird of prey, guarded by an earthen rampart and surrounded by rocky crags and tall forest trees. The only approach was a narrow pass rising steeply to the entrance gate. This made the position of the village secure and safe, and all attempts made by the invading Roman enemy to conquer the mountain settlement and enslave its fierce inhabitants had so far failed. In a defeated land, Caradoc's people and others like them lived a life of independence and freedom, growing their small crops in the rocky ground, keeping a few hardy sheep and goats, hunting and fishing in the mountain streams for their food, and often skirmishing fiercely with the neighbouring villages.

It was already late afternoon by the time Caradoc, limping and leaning heavily on the stout ash staff, made his way slowly home up the pass. He had parted company with John and the donkey some way below, to the keen relief of the donkey and with good wishes from John. Now he was hot, weary, and thirsty, and his ankle was painful again from the walking.

The first to see Caradoc was Brice, his father's old hunting-dog, a brown and white hound with tattered ears. He set up such a wild barking and threw himself with such tail-waving, slobbering joy upon the boy that the whole village came running to see the cause of the commotion. Caradoc's father, Tiernan, was among the foremost, a look of relief spreading across his bearded face. He had a haggard look, and Caradoc guessed that his father had spent much of the intervening time searching without food or sleep. Tiernan's eyes went at once to the injured foot, and he scooped up the boy in strong arms to carry him the last few yards to their own hut, with a hubbub of curious friends accompanying them.

Tiernan kicked the door firmly shut in the faces of others, and none dared to follow inside, for Tiernan was chieftain here, as his father before him. The hut was larger than most, two-roomed, built of wood with dried clay filling in the chinks, and furnished with rough but sturdy wooden furniture. A bright fire burned in the centre of the outer room, its smoke rising through a hole in the thatched roof. Caradoc's grandmother, Islean, started up from the couch where she had been resting after a sleepless night, and Caradoc saw a rare tear in her eye as she gave him a swift embrace. Next moment she was her usual brisk self, hastening to bring food and drink for her grandson and to tend his injury.

"The young cub looks half famished," remarked his father, who himself had eaten next to nothing since the alarm had been raised. "Now that he's back, I've a mind to kill and roast one of last year's fat lambs. Yes, a supper of roast mutton would go down very well, indeed."

He strode to the door and his voice could be heard shouting orders outside. "Not eaten or slept since you've been gone, he hasn't," confided Islean, examining the ankle, which Caradoc had stretched out before him on the couch. "He will want to know exactly what happened and how you survived the night. I am curious, myself. Where did you find shelter? And who bandaged your foot in this excellent way?"

Caradoc was beginning to explain, when the door burst open again and in came his brother Owain, a year older but half a head taller, with dark dishevelled hair and sturdy limbs. His fierce dark eyes brightened at the sight of his brother, and he flung himself down on the couch beside him.

"Brother - you're back! I have been searching up towards the top ridge, with Blair and Madoc, for hours! Where have you been? We thought a wolf had got you, or you'd been taken prisoner, or got mixed up with the invaders, even! Did you?"

Caradoc smiled at his brother's eagerness. "No. I never saw any invaders, nor even a raiding party from some other village. Just a house full of strange men, pottering about with donkeys and goats and vegetables."

Owain seemed disappointed, but Islean's face lit up with interest. "Tell us more, grandson, while I wrap your ankle again."

Caradoc was well into his tale, trying to remember every detail, when he suddenly became aware that the three of them were not alone. A tall, bearded figure in a long white robe had entered by the open door and stood regarding him with a frowning gaze from eyes as cold and grey as autumn hill fog. Caradoc's voice faltered and died away, as he realized that the man had been standing just outside the door for some minutes and had listened to every word of his account. This was Brychan, the Arch Druid, respected and feared by everyone in the village, the religious leader of the people and in some ways a more powerful figure even than Tiernan.

Brychan's mouth was compressed in a tight line, his voice when he spoke cold as a mountain stream. "Do not cut short your tale, son of Tiernan! Tell us more about these strange men. Did they pray to and worship some god of their own? Did they own no weapon and profess peace to all?"

"Y - yes." Caradoc had heard the men at their prayers, though he had not understood, and he had seen no weapon in their house. He dared not lie, though he sensed that his answer would sorely displease Brychan.

He was right. The Arch Druid's cold eyes glinted with anger. "Christian monks!" He spat out the words as though he tasted the venom of adders upon his tongue. "Those cowardly supporters of a new doctrine that opposes all that we have held sacred down through the years! Those woman-creatures who try to give the lie to the old beliefs! I have heard that these so-called holy men are now leaving their hermit's caves and banding together in these accursed houses! And you slept under their roof!"

Caradoc did not understand the reason for the tirade,

or how and why he had brought down the wrath of Brychan upon his head. He ventured to defend himself. "I - I didn't go willingly. I fought them - but I was injured. And they never harmed me - "

Brychan held up his hand and the boy fell silent. "Do not even speak of them! They and their kind are a spreading sore in the land, worse even than the enemy invaders who allow them to practice their arts! I have a mind to speak to Tiernan and bid him ride down and put a torch to their timbers when he has nothing better to do."

He turned and strode out of the building, his white robe swinging around him. After a moment, Owain, looking a little shaken, left the hut also, for only women and babes stayed indoors during the day.

Caradoc looked at Islean, whose face had grown pale.

"What did I do wrong, Islean? Who are these Christian monks?"

His grandmother shook her head, coming to sit beside him on the couch. Caradoc saw that her hands trembled a little. "I don't know. But somehow Brychan considers them a threat." She was silent for a while, then asked in a low voice, as though afraid the Druids might still be listening. "You say they were peaceful men, these - monks? Peaceful and kind?"

"Oh yes." Caradoc was beginning to recover himself. "They treated me well, even though I fought them. There was no weapon anywhere in the house, only womens' pots and pans and ladles."

He laughed.

Islean laid her hand upon his knee, a look in her eyes

Caradoc had never seen before. "No, don't pour too much scorn on people like these."

Caradoc's eyes opened wide in astonishment. "Why not? They are men of peace - weak men!"

Islean was silent for a moment, tucking a strand of greying hair under her kerchief. Then she said, "I know nothing of these men, but sometimes I think there must be a better way of living than this constant bloodshed, fighting, battles and killing."

Caradoc was round-eyed. "But what other way can there be? If we don't kill we shall be killed ourselves, sooner or later. How else can it be?"

Islean sighed. "I don't know. It's all I've ever known too. But sometimes I hate it all - and most of all, the Druids and their practices."

She looked fierce and suddenly much younger, and Caradoc caught a glimpse of the way she must have looked as a young girl, when his grandfather married her. He drew in his breath sharply, his eyes turning to the open doorway, through which showed the hillside with its circle of standing stones, in the centre of which burned the sacrificial fire, and higher still the grove of tall sacred oaks with their leaves tightly furled. They had always been there, but there was still something about them that brought a shiver to his spine.

He said fearfully, "But - Islean! The Druids! We dare not speak against them!"

"No. We dare not." Islean looked suddenly old again, old and defeated. "But it cannot be wrong to speak of other ways. Tell me more about this house of monks. You say there was a strange likeness on the wall?"

"Yes," said Caradoc, speaking in a low voice. "A

man dying on a wooden cross, nailed by his hands."

Owain's voice came from outside, loud and vibrant. "Islean! My father says the fat sheep is killed and dressed and ready to roast!"

Islean rose and busied herself with her cooking pots. But, as she worked, Caradoc saw her shake her head in wonder and heard her murmur "A man dying on a cross of wood! That's strange, that's very strange."

Chapter 4

Caradoc toiled slowly up the little knoll in the clearing, from which a clear view could be had of the pass and the valley beyond. Ahead of him, Owain bounded like a young goat and stood on the knoll, his sling swinging from his hand as he eagerly scanned the scene. He carried nothing but the sling, while Caradoc was weighed down by both their bows and arrows, as well as the string of game they had caught. His ankle was now quite well, and both boys took it for granted that Caradoc should be the one to carry the load.

A little stream, clear as crystal, gushed out from among tightly-furled brown fern fronds to splash and sparkle downhill where it would join the river below. Reaching the knoll, Caradoc threw down his burdens and sank down beside the stream, cupping his hands to drink from its clear coldness. He rested for a moment, looking up at his brother, who stood motionless scanning the valley with keen dark eyes.

"What are you looking for?"

Owain didn't answer at first, his sharp eyes darting

back and forth like a hawk's. Then he said, "Before you came up, wheezing and blowing like a broken-winded sheep, I thought I heard battle sounds. Shouting, and clashing of weapons. Perhaps it is our father and the rest."

Caradoc leapt to his feet and listened too. Their father had been gone on his latest adventure for more than seven days, and for the last day or two the boys had looked eagerly for his return. At first he thought he heard nothing but the gentle splashing of the stream and the evening twittering of nesting birds. Then came something else - a far-away tumult, the sound of many mens' voices raised together, and above it the clink of sword and spear on wood and metal. He turned to Owain.

"Yes. I hear it too."

Owain's face was alight with excitement. Every time his father set out in defence of his home, or an attacking foray against one of their neighbours, Owain longed wildly to join him. At intervals he pleaded his case, but so far in vain. Though he was so big and strong he had not yet seen fourteen summers, and his father considered that it must be another year at least before Owain went to battle.

"I see them!" he said suddenly, peering down the pass. "And listen - they're singing! They must have had good success. I'm going to meet them!"

He was off at once, bounding down the hillside in a series of springing leaps. Caradoc followed, leaving the game and hunting weapons where they were on the grass.

It was a triumphant procession that entered the mouth

of the pass, marching sturdily and singing one of the old battle songs, and beating their swords and shields together in the joy of victory. Tiernan marched to the fore, surrounded by his guard of honour, their faces and bodies painted with the blue warpaint so fearsome to their enemies. The eyes of the boys travelled eagerly from face to face as they neared the group. Every single warrior had returned in safety, with only a hacked shin here or a bound-up bloody arm there to show they had ever been in a battle. Their shields and weapons glinted bravely in the evening sun, though blunted and battered in places.

"They have a prisoner," said Owain suddenly. Caradoc held his breath. Yes, there was an extra man, young and tall, with a broken helmet and dented sword telling their own tale, marching in the rear between Rhain and Tavis, his hands bound behind his back.

The boys greeted their father and the others with enthusiasm, and then fell into line at the tail of the procession, gazing with curiosity at the prisoner. The captive was tall, taller than Brychan the Arch Druid, who was the tallest man in the village. He bore himself with dignity, his dark eyes gazing cynically around him, a stream of dried blood from a flesh-wound streaking his olive-skinned cheek. A bedraggled plume fluttered from his battered helmet, his shield, carried triumphantly by Rhain, bore the emblem of a fierce eagle, and he wore leather boots on his dusty feet.

This was no neighbouring Celt from a nearby village.

"Rhain!" hissed Caradoc, panting a little with the effort to keep abreast of the marching men. "This - this is one of the invaders, is it not?"

"Indeed it is!" answered the man cheerfully, twirling the short sword he had taken from the prisoner. "We came upon a bunch of them camping on the lower slopes, no doubt planning an attack, and fell on them before they could scarcely seize their weapons! Four we killed and the rest we put to rout - sending them fleeing back to their tents and their lowland towns. This one we captured - a fine prize indeed, with whom Brychan will be pleased!"

Caradoc saw the prisoner's lips twitch a little. He wondered if he understood and felt afraid, whether he guessed the fate that lay in store for him. It would be up to Brychan to decide, and whatever it was, Caradoc knew that his end would not be pleasant.

They had almost reached the village gate, and it seemed that the entire remaining population had turned out to watch the triumphal return of the warriors. Some of the boys and youths ran beside the prisoner and his guards, jeering and cat-calling. They would have thrown stones at him too, but for the fear of hitting their own fathers and brothers. The prisoner kept his dignity, staring straight ahead as they entered the village.

Before the fire within the sacred circle of stones, the Druids had gathered to greet the warriors, their white robes and flowing hair and beards giving the impression of a flock of fearsome birds of prey. The prisoner was marched straight up to Brychan and brought to a halt before the Arch Druid. The hubbub died away suddenly to an expectant hush.

"Of what race are you?" asked Brychan in stern tones.

The prisoner's head came up proudly and he answered in their own tongue.

"I am a Roman."

A little ripple of interest and scorn ran through the onlookers, which Brychan silenced with a lifted hand.

"An enemy invader of our land, rightly brought to justice," he said coldly.

There was silence for a moment, as though Brychan was considering the fate of the Roman. Behind him the sacred flame flickered and crackled, casting a ruddy glow over Brychan's cold features.

"Two nights ago I had a dream," he said at last. "I dreamed that at this year's feast of Beltane the gods would require a special sacrifice, and that when it was given they would prosper us this coming year with good success against our enemies. I have daily looked for the provision of a sacrifice that would please them, and now it is here."

He turned to Tiernan. "You have done well, Tiernan, and you will be rewarded. Guards, take this enemy and make him secure."

He turned away towards his own quarters near the sacred oak grove, and the other Druids followed. The silence of the villagers again broke up into a babble of excited talk. It had been some while since there had been a human sacrifice offered up among the circle of stones. It was especially favourable that it would take place at the feast of Beltane, and was surely a good omen for the coming year. The whole thing threw them into a mood of festivity, and preparations began for a great feast.

Owain had donned his father's helmet and was prancing round with Tiernan's spear and shield in his hands. Rhain and Tavis led the prisoner away between them, and for an instant Caradoc thought he saw a stricken look in the Roman's eyes. But the man's expression never changed, and he marched away between the two men with head held high.

There would be seven more sunsets and sunrises before the feast of Beltane.

Chapter 5

They housed the prisoner in one of the huts and fed him adequately; it would be dishonouring to the gods to offer them a half-starved, sickly sacrifice. After the first day, however, for the benefit of the guards who resented being confined in a dark hut during the fine spring weather, it was decided to lead the prisoner out each morning, hands bound, and tether him like a goat to a sturdy beech sapling at the edge of the village. The guards could then enjoy the fresh air and sunshine while having the prisoner always under their eye. Then there seemed so little possibility of his making a bid for escape that his hands were untied by day, and he was allowed to sit, tethered only by a stout rope round one ankle.

The Roman was an object of much curiosity to all the inhabitants of the village. They had heard tales of the fierce foreign soldiers who had come from over the water and taken over much of the low country, building strange hard roads and buildings of stone and making slaves of the people. Tiernan's warriors had been involved in more than one skirmish with the invaders, but this was the first time any of them had seen a Roman at close quarters.

Owain and Caradoc had taken charge of his breast-plate and helmet, and hung his shield and short straight sword in their own house, with their own weapons. Without them, the Roman looked much like any other young man, though tall and broad of shoulder.

"He is not so very different from us," said Caradoc, as they stood looking at him from a short distance that first morning.

"He is not as brave nor strong as Tiernan or any of our men," said Owain, quick to defend their father.

The Roman sat under his beech tree, arms resting on his knees, a look of resignation on his olive-skinned face. Owain had brought a handful of pebbles in his pouch, to throw at the prisoner in case they felt like a little sport. But somehow throwing stones at a bound man didn't seem as much fun as they might have thought. They walked round the man, examining him critically from all angles. One of the hunting dogs came up and sniffed at the prisoner's ankles, but instead of cuffing it or pushing it away as the boys might have expected, the man reached out and fondled its ears. After a moment the dog, whimpering with ecstasy, rolled over on its back and waved its legs in the air.

"The dog likes him," said Caradoc wonderingly.

"It well might - dogs don't know an enemy when they see one", said Owain. "A real man would have fetched that cur a cuff that made its ears ring. The fellow must be a weakling. No wonder he got captured."

"But our men say he fought bravely and we've seen for ourselves the great dent in his helmet," said Caradoc, striving to be fair.

"It doesn't take a brave man to get a great crack on the head with the flat of a sword," said Owain. "It just shows he's got a thick skull to survive it. If you ask me this prisoner lacks brains as well as courage."

The man spoke suddenly. "I have both brains and courage enough to take you across my knee and beat some manners into you, barbarian cub, given half a chance," he said softly, without turning his head.

The boys were startled. They had half-believed the prisoner to be somehow insensible to their remarks, like a dog or a sheep. To hear him speak their own tongue was something of a shock in itself, as well as the content of the remark.

Owain recovered himself quickly and stood stiffly, his eyes flashing.

"I am the chief's son, prisoner, and no barbarian cub! I have power to do you harm if you do not mind your tongue!"

"To someone destined for a Beltane sacrifice, that threat holds less terror than it might," said the prisoner drily. He raised a quizzical eyebrow and turned to look at them. "I am surprised your worthy father has not taught better manners to his sons."

"I - I - you - " To his chagrin, Owain found himself spluttering wrathfully, suddenly at a loss for words. He fingered the stones in his pouch as though he itched to hurl one at that cynical face, but turned and marched away instead.

"Ah - now I have offended him," said the Roman with mock regret.

Caradoc was a little puzzled. He felt that the prisoner

had somehow managed to get the better of them, without even lifting a finger or raising his voice. Suddenly curious, he asked, "How is it that you speak our tongue like one of ourselves?"

"Ah! I was well taught," said the prisoner, somehow managing to imply that neither Owain or Caradoc had been taught at all. "Also, I have spent a good part of my life in this chill and misty land."

Caradoc looked up at the blue sky with warm spring sunshine flooding the hillside.

"It's not - it's warm and sunny!"

The Roman laughed. "Compared to my land across the sea, this sun of yours has no heat in it. There, we have warmth that soaks into a man's very bones, and none of your rains, fogs, and biting winds."

Caradoc was suddenly consumed with curiosity. This man had seen the world, knew tongues other than his native one, could very likely give answers to many of the questions that so often filled Caradoc's mind. The boy sat down among the uncurling fronds of new bracken, inching a little nearer. Madoc and Blair, on guard duty, lolled nearby, half-asleep in the sun's warmth, and took no notice. The prisoner was tethered by a stout rope and had no weapon to cut himself free. Besides, they would be awake and upon him in a moment if by some means he contrived to loose himself. Madoc yawned, and Blair scratched himself, and both settled themselves into more comfortable positions.

Long into the afternoon the boy questioned and the man answered, one seeing in his memory and the other in his keen imagination stretches of shining blue water, dusty paths and olive-groves, white houses, and a laughing, merry, cultured people with smooth brown skins and dark eyes.

"You seem very friendly with that Roman dog," said Owain sourly, when they were eating their supper at their own hearth later in the day. "What could it be that you find to talk about with an enemy and an invader for a whole afternoon?"

"Many things," said Caradoc, taking a bite from a hunk of goat's flesh. "You would very likely not be interested if I told you. And the man has a name, you know. It is Lucius."

Chapter 6

The feast of Beltane was celebrated every year upon the first day of May. On that day, the women would let their normal small cooking fires die and go out. The only fire left burning would be the large one that burned always, the sacred flame in the stone circle near the grove of tall oaks. At mid-day the whole village would gather to watch the Druids perform their sacred rites, the chantings and casting of lots, the prophecies and predictions and finally the invoking of the gods and the great Mother Earth for the favours of fertility and health for human and animal alike protection from accident and danger, and victory in battle. After the sacrifice, usually a kid or lamb, had been consumed by the sacred flame, a member of each household would be given a brand from the fire with which to rekindle the cooking fire at his own hearth.

If the Roman, Lucius, knew details of the fate which awaited him, he showed no sign. As the days passed, Caradoc found himself drawn more and more to the company of the young man, whose experiences were endlessly fascinating to the boy. His short stay with the Christian monks in the lowlands had served to increase his curiosity about the outside world, and he found in Lucius a store of knowledge and information that held him spellbound for hours at a stretch. Neither of them mentioned the coming ordeal, until on the third day after the capture, Caradoc asked, his curiosity getting the better of him "Do you not fear death at the hands of the Druids?"

The young man stared first at the ground and then upwards to the mild blue of the sky, a strange expression in his dark eyes. He didn't answer for a moment. Then he said, "As a soldier, one learns to be prepared for death at any time. Yet death at the hands of one of these accursed priests is something I had not reckoned on." He looked at Caradoc with sadness in his eyes. "I think that, yes, my inquisitive young Celt, I do have a fear of death."

Caradoc was astonished. He had not really believed the Roman to be afraid, and to openly admit fear was something quite new to him. He said curiously, before he could stop himself, "Do you believe, then, in the Druid's teaching of an after life? Either one of bliss for those with whom the gods have found favour, or eternal punishment for others?"

Lucius answered with his sardonic smile. "You are as full of questions as an egg is full of meat, are you not?" He frowned, and his face became thoughtful. "Let me try to put into words what I believe. You see, I have had experience in my life of many teachings. There is the Emperor, whom most regard as a god himself. Then there are our old gods - Jupiter, Mars, Mercury, whom many of our older people still worship. I have heard too of Serapis and Isis, gods of Egypt, and of course there are you barbarians who coat yourselves in blue paint and worship sticks and stones and fire and trees." He gave a wry glance at the fire burning near the grove above them, with the flash of a white robe from the Druid who tended it.

"To sum it all up," he said, speaking slowly as though he had all the time in the world, "the only two gods who really held appeal for me were those of my two parents. My father's god on the one hand, and on the other, my mother's."

"And who were they?" asked Caradoc, making himself more comfortable in the grass.

"My father, being a soldier like myself - though he is now retired and farms a portion of land instead - was a devoted follower of Mithras. Mithraism is an excellent religion for a soldier, with its emphasis on discipline, strength and valour. I myself took part in the taurabolem, where a man enters a deep pit dug in the earth and covered by a grating. Then a bull is led onto the grating, its throat cut with a swift thrust and its blood runs down to drench the soldier below. It is said to confer great strength."

Caradoc eyed the Roman's impressive biceps. "It seems to have worked with you!"

Lucius laughed. "Well, I don't know. Maybe I am by nature a muscular man. Who can tell in these matters? All I know is that, as a little child, I listened intently at my mother's knee when she told me tales of her god, but the moment the soldiers appeared and spoke of the glories of following Mithras, I had no attention for any but them."

"And who was your mother's god?"

A softer look had come into the Roman's eyes. "He was the Lord Christ."

Caradoc sat upright with a start. "The Lord Christ? Is that the same as the Christian God?"

Lucius nodded. "Yes. Why, what do you know of him?"

Caradoc clasped his hands about his bare, scratched legs. "Once, some time ago," he said slowly - it was not yet a month but already it seemed a long time - "I was thrown from my pony in the lower forest, and a man came and tended me and took me to his home. Afterwards, Brychan was angry and told me it was a place of Christian monks."

"Really?" said Lucius with a flicker of interest. "I had not realised that you were a travelled young man. Or that there was a gathering of Christian holy men nearby. How did you like these monks, and their way of life?"

"It was - strange," said Caradoc slowly, trying to remember the impressions he had formed. "Their home was full of many strange things. There was, on a table, a thick, flat thing of many sheets between covers, which the monks looked at a great deal - "

"A book," said the Roman. "Full of writings. Probably the Scriptures, or part of them."

"Scriptures?" Caradoc was puzzled. "Writings?" Then he remembered the long sharp quills and black liquid one of the monks had used to make scratching marks upon another flat sheet.

"There was another strange thing," he said, and tried to explain about these.

"Quills," said Lucius. "And ink. We would use a

41

stylus. But both have the same purpose. To write - to make marks for others to read. And before you ask me what read means, I will tell you."

Caradoc listened spellbound to what the prisoner was telling him - that legends, accounts, remedies, tales of the world and everything that lived or grew in it, and of the sea and stars - anything that could be spoken or sung could also be written down and recorded and read again.

"And can only monks read?" he asked wistfully, thinking how wonderful it would be to have all that knowledge in his mind and skills at his fingertips.

Lucius laughed again. "Oh no. I can read myself. Anyone can, if they are taught."

Caradoc thought for a moment, holding his breath. Then he said, hardly daring to hope, "Could I, too - learn to read?"

Lucius looked at him with the smile that was cynical but not unkind. "Undoubtedly. I would say that you are about as intelligent a young barbarian as any other I have come across, in this land or elsewhere."

Caradoc scarcely heeded these last words, though they were high praise indeed. He said breathlessly, "And could you - could you teach me?"

Lucius gave a short laugh. "Well, I doubt not that I could. But I'm afraid our course of study would be cut short, come the first of May. But, certainly, we could make a start. You would learn rapidly, if I'm any judge. It might even prove a challenge to see how much progress you could make in the limited time we have."

He reached up and broke a twig from his beech tree which he handed to Caradoc, then broke one for himself and smoothed the dusty ground with one booted foot.

"These will be our writing instruments. Now, you understand that the language I teach will be the one used also in the writings at your house of Christian monks. I doubt that this barbaric tongue of yours has ever been written, or could be. Let us start with the alphabet - so!"

He made marks in the dust with the stick, repeated a letter over until Caradoc had memorized it, then rubbed out the marks and invited the boy to make them for himself. Another followed, and another. Caradoc was totally absorbed, quickly committing to memory one mark after another. Nothing in his life had ever fascinated him so much.

The lesson was rudely interrupted by Owain, who appeared hot and flushed before them and demanded to know what they were doing.

"I am learning to read, and to write," said Caradoc with pride. "Already I know the names of many letters and can write them. Why don't you come and learn with me?"

"Pah! I've better things to do than sit playing in the dust with sticks!" said Owain scornfully. He shuffled his feet in the patch of dust, obliterating the last letters they had formed, threw a scornful look at them both and ran off laughing.

Caradoc was annoyed. "He thinks of nothing but hunting and battles!"

"As do many," said Lucius. "And not only you barbarians! Also, he is jealous of his brother spending so much time in the company of another. Never mind, we have made good progress. You would quickly rise to the top of any class in Rome! It is enough for today."

Caradoc found himself strangely reluctant to tear

himself from the company of the Roman prisoner. He sighed with regret, and tried to think of something else to keep the conversation going. "In the monk's house," he said "there was another thing - "

Lucius groaned and put his head between his hands. "And it was a strange thing also, I suppose?"

Caradoc ignored the sarcasm. "Yes. A likeness of a man, dying on a cross of wood."

"Ah." The Roman was suddenly serious.

"Do you know what it means?"

"I do."

"Then tell me."

"I see I will have to, if there is to be any rest for me! The cross - that is our Roman method of execution for criminals."

"Then the man was a criminal?"

"Some believed that. Myself, I have heard other accounts, and I cannot believe so. A fool maybe, but not a wicked man."

"But who was he?"

"He was the Christian God - the one they called Jesus."

"The one your mother follows?"

"Yes."

"But - " Caradoc frowned in perplexity. "He was a man, and a dying one. Did he not die on that cross? If so, then how can a dead man be a god?"

"He did die, but his followers claim he rose to life again on the third day, leaving behind an empty tomb. They say his spirit lives still in the hearts of those who love him, and that through him many great and powerful works are done. They say he has power to heal the sick, raise the dead and save souls for all eternity."

His voice shook suddenly. Caradoc felt himself strangely stirred by the words, but he said, "I thought you said you were no follower of his?"

"Maybe I will yet be," said Lucius, his voice still bearing a trace of emotion and quite unlike his usual sardonic tone. "My mother has prayed much, I know, that I will embrace the teachings of the Lord Christ. Maybe her prayers will yet be answered, even at this late hour."

Chapter 7

It was the last day of the old month, and all day long there had been a bustle of activity in the mountain village, with a slaughtering and dressing of sheep and goats for next day's roasting, a mixing and stirring and baking of the choicest delicacies the women could produce for the festivities of next day. An extra supply of firewood faggots had been cut and carried in, piled ominously near to the sacred flame.

Caradoc watched all the preparations with a sick feeling in the pit of his stomach, all too aware of the sinister overtones to this seemingly merry occasion. He kept away from the prisoner altogether, not knowing how to look into the eyes of a man who on the morrow was doomed to die a violent death at the hands of his people. They had continued their lessons over the preceding days, with Caradoc a quick and eager pupil and Lucius an able teacher. The expression of the Roman had remained unfathomable, but as the fateful day drew nearer, the boy had sensed a new nervousness in his movements, had heard a deep troubled sigh or two when it seemed that no-one was noticing, and once he thought he saw the gleam of tears in the sardonic dark eyes. But the Roman said nothing more either of his coming fate or of his own feelings, and Caradoc did not ask. He would like to have offered words of comfort, but anything he thought of saying sounded false even to his own mind, and besides, what comfort was there to offer to a condemned man? He concentrated instead on the Latin figures marked out in the dust by the beech pointer, greedily adding each day to his rapidly expanding store of knowledge.

Yet when Owain, who had been jealous of his brother's friendship with the young Roman, said gloatingly that evening, "This will be the best Beltane ever, I think!" He jumped up hurriedly, overturning his bowl of mutton broth, and hurried out of the hut, finding his eyes suddenly full of stinging tears. He ran from the village and away into the tangled woodland, where, with a nightingale singing its piercingly sweet song from a hazel thicket nearby, he flung himself face down and sobbed for the imminent loss of a friend.

Everyone retired as soon as darkness fell, to refresh themselves ready for the excitements of the next day. Caradoc could not sleep. Long after steady breathing and gentle snores told him that the other members of his family were fast asleep, he tossed restlessly on his bed of boughs and animal skins. Out in the prison hut, closely guarded, Lucius lay helpless and alone, the hours and moments of his life fast ebbing away. Did he think, lying there, of his retired soldier father, of his gentle mother, of the sloping sunny olive-groves of his homeland or the marching men of the legion to which he had belonged? Thinking of the Roman's keen mind, his strong muscular body and the friendship he had offered to an unknown and ignorant son of his captors, Caradoc had to stifle the sobs again. Since returning to the hut and retiring to bed, a wild idea had been suggesting itself to his mind, but the mere thought of putting it into action made his limbs turn to jelly and his stomach seem to turn over with fear. If he could succeed in carrying it out and was discovered, the punishment would be severe indeed. He would disgrace not only himself in the eyes of the Druids but his father and all his family too. It was unthinkable.

But the idea of the bright blood of Lucius spilling out over Brychan's sharp curved blade was unthinkable too. Caradoc had always been sickened even by the sacrifice of a lamb or kid. He tossed and turned, as hot as though stricken with sudden fever, imagining the sardonic eyes of the Roman glazing in death like the eyes of a speared stag. As the darkness deepened, a clearer resolution began to form. It was past midnight when he judged that everyone in the village except the guards must be asleep. Sick and shaking, but with a new determination in his heart he rose quietly, took his sharp skinning knife and stole from the hut.

Keeping to the dark shadows around the dwellings Caradoc crept silently from hut to hut until he reached the one where the prisoner lay, with Tavis and Cynan lolling against the doorposts, no more than half awake themselves. In fact, a bubbling snore from the open mouth of Tavis proved that he was indeed asleep at his post.

Caradoc flitted, a silent shadow among larger

flickering shadows cast by the ever-burning fire beyond, to the back of the prison hut. He knew the exact place where Lucius was tied to a stout post, and felt cautiously along the wooden wall until he came to a slight crack between the timbers. His hands steadier now, he carefully picked away some of the dried clay between the chinks until a hole big enough to slip a knife through appeared. He dared not speak a word, but the tiny scraping sounds had roused Lucius, who got to his feet and came close to the place. When Caradoc passed the sharp knife through the space it was taken at once by an unseen hand. Holding his breath, Caradoc retreated to the trees at the edge of the sleeping village and waited. It seemed that Cynan, too, had finally given in to weariness, and had dropped off for a moment, for very soon, making no sound on dry beaten earth, the Roman stepped softly from the door between the two waiting guards and ran to join the boy where he stood. He would have whispered his thanks, but Caradoc seized his hand and led him quickly further into the shelter of the trees.

"Don't go by the pass - that's the way they'll follow when they miss you. I'll show you a path."

He led the way over the rim of the surrounding earthwork and plunged into the tangled woodland beyond the clearing. They pushed their way swiftly along the narrow pathway for some time before pausing to draw breath.

"Now, this path will bring you out of the forest lower down towards the valley," said Caradoc in a breathless whisper. "After that, I don't know where you should go. Follow the river, maybe. But in any case, get as far away as you can before daylight."

The Roman seized the boy's hands in both of his. "I will not forget what you did. There, take back your knife, or questions may be asked. And take this also, with my heartfelt thanks."

He wore a broad gold ring on one finger, which he now pulled off and pressed into the boy's hand. Next moment, with a lift of the hand, the Roman was gone, his dark shape turning a bend in the path and vanishing among the trees.

Caradoc drew in a long breath, hardly daring to believe that his plan had worked. He felt the ring still warm from the Roman's finger and put it into the pouch at his belt. If the Roman's escape was not discovered until morning there was a good chance that he would get clean away.

It remained to return unseen to his own bed. The sick, shaking feeling returned as he retraced his steps to the village. If his part in the escape was discovered it would go ill with him, for the Druids had set much store by this Beltane sacrifice. But the village still slept against the ruddy glare of the banked fire. Before the empty prison hut, the guards snored. Not even a dog stirred or moved as he stole back to his own hut. Just for one moment, though, he thought he saw a shadow move up near the sacred stones, but it could have been caused by a flicker of flame. No one challenged him, and he breathed a sigh of relief as he entered his home and saw that all the family still slumbered. Within moments of lying down upon his own bed he was sound asleep.

The sky was just beginning to show streaks of light and the first blackbird was beginning his morning song from the top of the tallest oak when the chief's household was awakened by pounding feet and a great hammering on the door. Next moment Cynan and Tavis burst in with the news of the escape of the prisoner.

Tiernan sprang from his bed with a bound, and left his house to investigate the situation and organize pursuit. In a matter of minutes some of the young men, accompanied by their eager hounds, were spreading through the woods in search of the escaped Roman, while others clattered on horseback down the pass.

The rest of the village had gathered to noisily discuss this development, Caradoc and Owain among them. There was astonishment and speculation when the short rope-end was found, cut by a sharp knife.

"Who could have done it?" asked Owain excitedly, as the two boys made their way back to their hut in search of breakfast.

Caradoc shrugged. "Could have been anyone, I suppose."

But he thought that his brother threw him a sharp glance from his keen dark eyes.

Half-way through the morning, when the men had come back empty-handed, a council was called at the Stones. Brychan's face wore the most angry expression anyone had ever seen. Caradoc inwardly shuddered as he looked at the dark cruel countenance.

"I have consulted the gods, and they are angry," said the Arch Druid in stern cold tones. "Someone in this village has cut the bonds of the prisoner and set him free, the act of a traitor to our people and to our land. Until that one is found and brought to justice, no sacred fire will be allowed to kindle your cooking fires. They must stay cold and dead. Only the substitution of the guilty person as a Beltane sacrifice will appease the anger of the gods."

Everyone gasped at the harshness of this judgment, and glanced at each other in horrified amazement. Caradoc felt the colour drain from his face and his heart began to hammer hard against his ribs. The village depended on fire for its cooking purposes, for keeping at bay the wolves and wild boars that roamed the forests and for warmth against the mountain chill. A subdued murmur broke from the people, but Brychan's word was law, and none, not even Tiernan, dared oppose him.

"The gods will help us seek out the guilty one" said Brychan, raising his hand for silence. "We will draw lots. Bring a cooking pot and small stones."

A cooking vessel was brought, and several small stones counted carefully into it, one stone for each household in the village. Those near enough to see noticed that all of the stones were white except for one black pebble. The household that drew the black stone would be shown to be sheltering the guilty party under its roof.

There was an air of gathering tension as, one by one, the heads of the households stepped up and drew a stone from the pot, held high by one of the Druids so that they could not see into it. Five or six men drew white stones, to sighs of relief from their families. Caradoc bit his lip, keeping his head down as the men went up one by one, feeling the tension almost unbearable. Then there was a sudden gasp from Owain, followed by a groan from the assembled villagers. Tiernan, the last in line, had stepped up to take his turn and had returned ashen-faced and holding the black stone.

Chapter 8

Almost before Caradoc had time to realize what had happened, his arm was seized in a tight grip and his brother's voice was hissing in his ear. "Quick - back to our house!" Caradoc found himself hurried back to their hut, while Tiernan stood with a stunned look and the villagers broke out into a dismayed babble of discussion about this latest development.

"There's no time to lose," said Owain in a low urgent voice. "In another moment they'll be trying to decide which one of us did it. Pretend we're going in at our own door and then slip round and into the trees."

Breathless, Caradoc found himself propelled past their own door and concealed by the house, across the clearing and into the undergrowth.

"I know you did it," panted Owain as he pushed and tugged at his brother, who felt sluggish with shock. "I guessed from the start. You've got to get away! Go - and don't come back! Brychan will have you killed once he works it out!"

"But - " Caradoc's brain seemed paralysed. "Where

shall I go?"

"Anywhere - just go! To the house of monks - they 'll take you in! I'll cover for you, to gain time. But go!"

He gave Caradoc a last push away from him and then doubled back, dodging and twisting to reach the village again before either of them was missed.

For a moment Caradoc just stood gazing after him, still numb with shock. Events had happened at such speed that he could scarcely take them in. But he knew that what his brother had said was true. His very life would be in danger when Brychan found out what he had done, as find out he surely would.

A clamour of voices sounded faintly from beyond the earthworks, and Caradoc came suddenly to life. At any moment angry white-robed figures could appear, searching the woods for him, and demanding his life as a penalty. He turned and dived away through the bushes, running through brambles, gorse and undergrowth, never noticing that his legs were soon scratched and bleeding, splashing through streams and zig-zagging among the trees, his heart thumping and his breath coming in short gasps. Not until he was deep into the woodland, where the trees grew so thick and tall that the sun scarcely penetrated, and no undergrowth grew between them, did he slacken his speed a little.

There was no noise of pursuit, and his feet made no sound on the soft thick layer of leaf-mould. The only sounds were his own laboured gasps. The terror had subsided a little, but a feeling of grief was taking its place. He was guilty of a sin against the gods, had run away to escape his punishment and would never dare go back. His action of the night had settled his fate once and for all. Strangely enough it was Islean who was uppermost in his mind, Islean who had guided his first steps, fed and nursed and scolded him, stitched his tunics and leggings and boots and shared with him her longing for a better way of life. He knew that Islean would grieve for him, and the thought caused the hot tears to fill his eyes and blur his vision. He dashed them away with a grimy fist, and his feet pounded silently on the soft earth.

Almost without thinking he had found the way he had been brought with John and the donkey when they had despatched him homeward after his visit to the house of monks. He had no real wish to go there again, but Owain's desperate words "Go - anywhere -the house of monks - just go!" echoed in his mind. They had taken him in then, full of fight and ungrateful as he had been, and surely they would again. The only alternative was to take his chances in the open, where, even if he was not found, he knew he would be hard put to it to survive alone.

He had slowed almost to a walk, breathing hard while he got his second wind. The dreary thought had come to him that perhaps it might be preferable to die alone than join with those strange, peaceable and kindly men who were so different to his own wild turbulent clan. He did not belong there. But another thought followed - that he did not quite belong with his own people either. He could hunt and fight like them if he had to, but that wasn't really all there was to life. He realized suddenly, all in a moment, that the most satisfactory time in his life had been the past few days, talking over a variety of topics with the Roman and being taught by him to read and spell and write.

A new thought struck him, one that made him catch his breath and almost stop in his tracks. Maybe the monks would continue the teaching that Lucius had begun. Maybe they would even introduce him to the mysteries of those books that had so fascinated him, though he had not then known what they were. Almost unconsciously, remembering the sharp marks made by black ink on a clear sheet, he broke into a run again, feeling new strength return to his limbs.

The afternoon shadows were beginning to lengthen across the ground when at last Caradoc emerged from the thick forest and into more open land, where birch trees grew slim and tall with a carpet of bluebells beneath them. He was very tired. Weariness pressed on him like a heavy weight, making his feet drag and his head ache. He peered ahead with hot, prickling eyes, trying to remember where the monk's house had been.

He saw it at last, a dark low shape against the wood's edge, facing down the valley. A thin curl of smoke rose from the roof - the monks must be cooking their supper. Caradoc had eaten nothing that day and was suddenly ravenous, quickening his footsteps towards it.

The first living thing he saw was the donkey, tethered by a stake to graze the tender sweet grass at the fringe of the woods. It turned its head to look at him with a long wisp hanging from its jaws, and Caradoc could have sworn it remembered carrying him trussed up upon its back. At any rate, when he put out a hand to touch it, it backed off hurriedly and turned its hindquarters ready to kick, as though to discourage him from any notion he might have of trying again to climb upon its back. There was a tethered goat with a kid, but no sign of human life.

Caradoc passed the vegetable plots, green with hopefully sprouting plants, and hammered at the heavy wooden door. It was opened by the young monk who had once brought him breakfast, whose jaw dropped a little at the sight of him. Caradoc realized that he must look a startling sight, with legs and arms scratched and blood-stained, his hair wild and face streaked with dirt, tears and sweat. He said hoarsely, "John?" and the young monk recovered himself at once.

"I'll fetch him," he said, and hurried away.

Brother John came bustling in from the back regions, his face a study of surprise at the sight of his dejected young visitor. Then he smiled. "I do believe it is our fierce young eaglet from the hills, come home to roost! Come, sit down and I'll bring you food and drink, and you can tell me what has made you return."

Over gulped mouthfuls of bread and cheese and goat's milk, Caradoc blurted out his sorry tale. Brother John listened gravely, nodding now and then. He seemed to understand all about the Druids and their customs. He said, when Caradoc paused for breath, "So, you have come to us for sanctuary. Well, we will give it to you, of course. Do they know where you have fled?"

Caradoc shook his head. "Only my brother Owain, and he won't tell."

Remembering suddenly the hatred in the voice and eyes of Brychan when he talked of the monks, he realized for the first time that by coming here for refuge he was perhaps endangering the lives of the monks too. As though he could read the boy's thoughts, Brother John said quickly, "We have no fear of the Druids and their false gods. Our true Lord Christ is stronger than they, and we are under his good protection."

Caradoc's eyes turned to the woodcarving showing the suffering man on the cross. "Him?" Brother John shook his head. "No - not in the way you mean. That is but a clever likeness carved by man, a symbol to help us remember. Our real Lord cannot be seen by human eye, but nonetheless is real and powerful and very much alive. With him, we need have no fear of what men can do to us, for they cannot harm our spirit - our inner self - which cannot die and which goes on for ever."

He put out a hand to the boy, noticing suddenly that Caradoc was swaying with weariness. "To your bed, I think."

Later, lying on the same pallet he had occupied on his first visit, Caradoc heard the pattering of rain on the roof. He pulled the covering over his head and wept as he had never wept before. For Islean and his strong father Tiernan, for Owain who had dominated and taunted and often bullied him for all of his life, but who at the end had risked his own life to save Caradoc's. He wept for the life in the mountain village which was all he had ever known, and which was now behind him for ever.

Chapter 9

Rain continued to fall for the next two days, a warm, life-bringing rain that caused the trees to burst their buds, and brought grass, wheat and weeds alike springing into vigorous new growth from the damp earth.

On the third day the rain stopped and the sun shone warmly again. Brother Dafyd, the monk in charge of the wheat and barley crops, appeared soon after breakfast with his garment tucked up and two hoes in his hand, one of which he handed to Caradoc.

Caradoc took it, slightly puzzled. For two days he had stayed mainly indoors, partly because of the rain and partly because he half-expected a party from his village, sent by the Druids, to appear at the monks' gate in search of him. But no-one came, and this morning he had planned to take his sling and stones and hunt rabbit and partridge in the lower woodland. Shut up indoors he felt like a caged wild thing, pacing about or lying on his pallet, watching the monks at their womens' work but not speaking to any except John. At times he almost wanted to flee back to the woods, but the thought of

Brychan's cold angry face and cruel grey eyes restrained him. Beltane was past, but the Druids' curved blades would be still keen and sharp, and their feelings of vengeance sharper still. His only safety, irksome though it seemed, lay here with the men of Christ.

He looked at the hoe put into his hand with a frown of puzzlement, which deepened as Dafyd beckoned him to follow out of doors. Stepping into the sunshine he realized with a shock that the burly monk intended him to help hoe the barley.

Caradoc had never held a hoe in his life, or anything much other than a spear or a bow. He grasped it clumsily while Dafyd, speaking slowly, first pointed to the growing barley shoots, then indicated the couch-grass, fat-hen and other weeds springing between the rows, and showed him how to root them out with a quick dig and turn of the hoe.

For a few seconds Caradoc was stunned into silence, and even tried to imitate Dafyd, who was already moving smoothly along a row, despatching weeds with a steady deft flick of the wrist. It looked easy, but in Caradoc's hands the hoe felt awkward and clumsy, and try as he might he could not root out the weeds in the same way. Instead finding that far too often the hoe seemed to aim for the barley itself or miss altogether, and that he was soon left many yards behind.

Sweat broke out all over his body and indignation rose in his heart. He felt bitterly humiliated. How Owain would laugh to see the ludicrous figure of his brother scratching in the dirt like a village woman! And he was the son of a chief! Suddenly he flung the hoe far across the barley field and marched across it himself, not caring that he trampled down the rows of hopeful plants and taking no notice of Dafyd's shout of protest.

Caradoc flung himself past the outbuildings and past where the livestock grazed at the forest's edge, deep into the woodland. In the shade of the trees his hot cheeks cooled a little, and his feelings of humiliation were gradually replaced by one of grief and frustration. He did not fit in here, and dared not return to his own people. The hot tears stung his eyelids and he flung himself down on a grassy knoll and sobbed in hard unhappy gasps.

A rabbit hopped from a bramble patch and looked at him, but he had left his sling behind and there was no stone handy. The sun was high above the trees, and the ache inside told him that it must be time for the monks' noon meal. There was nothing to do but to return to them if he wished to eat.

He presented himself, grimy and dishevelled, at the long table where the monks were finishing their barley broth and bread. To his chagrin, nothing was offered to him, and in a few more moments the table was being cleared. He saw Brother Dafyd give him a steely glance with a tight compression of the lips, and stared boldly back. "Where is my food?"

The man shrugged, indicating that he could not understand the boy's language, though Caradoc saw that he understood very well. He felt his temper rise. He sought out Brother John, and asked rudely "Why am I not given food?"

The monk shook his greying head a little sadly. "You have much to learn, my son, if you would stay with us. Dafyd told me you threw down your hoe and marched away when asked to help. That kind of attitude we cannot tolerate. If you wish to stay with us, and be fed, you must take your share of the work."

Caradoc felt his mouth fall open a little. He had never been required to do anything more strenuous than sharpening an arrow or a spear in preparation for a day's deer hunting or pursuing wild boar with the men. He felt indignation rise again. "But I am a chief's son!"

John shook his head. "Not here. Here, we are all equal with Christ our head. Everyone must bear a hand with the needful tasks. Since you have joined us you must learn to work also."

Caradoc felt the indignation ebb away. "But I can't do it - the hoeing! Already I have blisters on my hands." He held out his palms pathetically.

The monk smiled. "You will learn, and your hands will harden." He paused, seeing the deflated look on the boy's face and the sag of his shoulders, and added "A day is not all used for work, you know. Maybe there will be time for study too. I have seen you look at our quills and parchments."

Caradoc's head jerked up, his hurt pride forgotton. "Oh, could I? Already I can read and write a little! Will you teach me more? I will take my share of the work, I promise!"

So it was that the days quickly fell into a pattern, in which Caradoc quickly learned not only to turn his hand to hoeing and cultivating, mending fences and preparing food, but also to such menial tasks as cleaning the donkey's stall and milking the nanny-goat. It was all made worth-while though, by those other times when Brother John himself instructed the boy in reading, spelling, writing and figuring, in which both were amazed at the rapid progress he made.

The ability to read opened up a whole new world to the boy, into which he threw himself as a thirsty man plunges into water. He found he could happily spend hour after hour poring over the few precious books at the monks' house, eagerly delving into the treasures to be found between their pages.

Life slipped into a routine more quickly than he could have imagined. There were still times when he was desperately homesick, but these became fewer as days passed by into months. The peaceful labour of his life filled him with a certain satisfaction though he was often exhausted by the end of the day, being required to rise before first light for early morning prayers and work before breakfast, with more work punctuated by more prayers right through the day. The monks were a different kind of men from any he had ever known, devoting their lives to simple things, never fighting and killing but instead reaching out their hands to those in need, building and modelling their lives on the Christian God they called Jesus.

Caradoc had read much about Jesus in the books of Scriptures. Gradually he came to understand how this God and Creator of the world had come from Heaven to live as a man among other men, to do good to all and then to offer himself freely as a sacrifice for all men, taking their sins upon himself and bearing their punishment. Reading of Jesus made something stir in Caradoc's own heart, a kind of longing that nothing else had ever inspired. It was almost mid-summer, and the barley was fast turning from green to gold, when Brother John quietly asked one day, as they sat together over their studies, "What do you think of the Lord Christ, my son?"

Caradoc thought for a moment before he replied, hearing through the open window the call of a cuckoo. He felt the longing well up within his heart, and said at last, "I believe Him to be the one true God, the only one with power to change mens' lives. I would like to be a follower of His. Is this possible?"

Brother John nodded, and explained that the love and mercy of Jesus extended to everyone, of every tribe and race and nation, no matter what their former beliefs and teachings had been, if they would truly turn to Him.

Soon afterwards, Brother John had baptized Caradoc in the spring nearby, dipping water and pouring it over the boy's head in the name of the Father and the Son and the Holy Ghost. There was talk of Caradoc himself joining the monks permanently when he was older. The idea held appeal to the boy, though sometimes deep down inside he was not quite sure. For the time he was content to read the Latin tongue, to question his teacher and to write with a quill upon the parchment.

The days lengthened, and when the barley and wheat were ripe and golden, Caradoc took his turn with the sickle and later in carrying the bundles of corn home. When all was gathered in they had winnowed the grain, which now lay in a fragrant heap in the monks' granary ready for making good barley bread for the coming year, and thanks had been offered to God for a good harvest. Now it was time to plough the land again, so that the winter frosts could break it down ready for the next year's crops.

Ploughing was hard work, as Caradoc found on the October day that he first tried it. At dusk, he straightened up and rubbed his stiff back, sweat streaking his forehead and every muscle aching from pulling the plough. Behind him, Dafyd stretched wearily too, and wiped sweaty hands on his garment. He hooked a leather bucket from where it hung on the fence, offered it to Caradoc and drank from it himself. Both rested for a moment, surveying the dark furrows of freshly-turned earth stretching away across the field.

"We shall finish by nightfall, God willing," he said optimistically. "We make a good team at the plough, you and I."

Caradoc grinned and agreed, thinking how far away it seemed that day when the monk had first thrust a hoe into his unwilling hand. It was almost dark when the ploughing was finished, the last line of golden stubble turned under rich dark soil. Caradoc and the burly monk were both tired out, but satisfied with the results of their toil. "I think we've done as good a job as any ox or plough-horse could," said Dafyd, giving a comradely slap to the boy's shoulder as they put away the plough and turned indoors. "And I do believe there's a nip in the air. I think we're going to have our first frost."

Caradoc was exhausted; during supper and prayers his head nodded over and over again, and he was asleep the moment he lay down upon his pallet bed in the small room he shared with one or two of the younger monks. He slept deeply, and dreamed of ploughing a steep field with a braying donkey in harness beside him.

Sometime in the small hours of the morning, he stirred and murmured a little. The dream had persisted and seemed very real, he could actually hear the loud braying of the donkey and a thumping and banging as though it was kicking its stall. He opened his eyes. The donkey's braying was real and so were the other noises. Something was going on out there in the stable, but he was far too tired to go out to investigate. He groaned and turned over, pulling the covering over his head. It was still pitch dark, not yet time for the bell to ring to summon him to morning prayers. Whatever was the matter with that donkey?

He was half-asleep again, dimly aware that the donkey's noise had been replaced by a murmur of human voices in the region of the entrance. Then John was calling his own name "Caradoc! Caradoc! Are you awake? Get up and come here to me!"

Caradoc groaned again and struggled to his feet, sleepily pulling his tunic over his head. Half-asleep still, he staggered out into the large main room, where Brother John had lit a rush dip and was talking in low tones with a stranger who stood just inside the doorway. Caradoc stopped in the middle of a huge yawn and his jaw stayed open in amazement. The newcomer was his brother Owain.

Chapter 10

Owain stood just inside the open door, poised uneasily upon the threshold as though prepared to take flight at any moment. Caradoc's first impression was one of slight shock at his brother's wild dishevelled appearance, his long tangled hair and darting restless eyes, until he remembered that he himself must have looked much the same before the monks had taken a pair of shears to his own hair, insisted on regular washings in cold water and won his trust.

Brother John stood holding the rushlight, which cast flickering shadows in the draught from the open door. "Your brother has come to see you, Caradoc," he said calmly.

Caradoc blurted out the first words which came into his mind. "But why in the middle of the night?"

Owain scowled fiercely. "It was day time when I started, but I couldn't find my way to this place. I wandered about the woods trying to find the path for the best part of the day. Then when I did get here, it was pitch dark and I took the wrong doorway - ended up in a stable with a donkey! The stupid brute nearly kicked the stall to pieces - kicked me as well - look!"

He pulled aside one legging to show a large reddened patch, swollen and rapidly bruising, where the donkey's flailing hooves had found a mark. There were other bruises and marks on his hand and arms, where he had tried to fend the hooves off while fumbling in the darkness to find the doorway again. In spite of himself, Caradoc felt his lips twitch. He could well imagine the scene in the stable, with a startled donkey, whose temper was unpredictable at the best of times, disturbed from its slumber.

Brother John said quickly, "I'll get something to put on that to reduce the swelling."

He set the light on a chest and went to the little room where he kept his ointments, lotions and remedies. The brothers looked at each other, Owain still poised as though for a quick escape, Caradoc a little puzzled. "What did you want of me to come searching for me?"

"It's Islean," said Owain, pulling his legging into place. "She's very sick - she's had a fever for five or six days now. She coughs often, and tosses from side to side. Tiernan thinks she is dying. He sent me for you, because for the last two days she's talked of you and called out your name. Tiernan thinks it will ease her passage into the next world if you came. So I promised I would try to find you."

The thought of Islean dying made Caradoc feel as though he had been thumped hard in the stomach. He said, "But - I thought I could never come back -because of Brychan. Will not Brychan want me killed?"

"Brychan is dead himself," said Owain, counting on

his fingers "has been dead - let's see - almost since the last new moon. Druce is Arch Deacon now, and Tiernan has more influence with him than with Brychan. Anyway, our father thought it would be safe for you to come home now."

"I see."

Caradoc was silent for a moment, weighing up the implications. The quiet life of the monks had become his own way now, and the thought of returning to the rough, undisciplined life of the village gave him a strange pang. What if his father required him to stay? Could he give up this new way of life and return to the old?

But then, there was Islean, deathly sick and calling out for him. His mind was quickly made up. "I'll come," he said.

Owain looked vastly relieved. "Good. Then let's be gone at once. This strange place makes me uneasy."

John had returned with the salve, which he applied to Owain's bruised places. Owain flinched at the monk's touch, as though he feared some strange power might be transmitted from one to the other, and drew away as quickly as he could.

"You had better rest for a while and start in the morning," said the monk quietly.

Caradoc saw suddenly through the open doorway that the dark night sky was just beginning to be tinged with the first rays of the new dawn. At the same moment, the bell for morning prayers began to ring, causing Owain to start violently.

"It's all right," said Caradoc quickly. "I'll come right away. Just let me get my boots and leggings."

He padded away barefoot to the sleeping-room. At

the doorway Brother John stopped him with a hand on the boy's arm. "God go with you, my son. Return to us if you can. Remember our doors will always be open to you."

Caradoc felt a lump rise in his throat. It would not be easy leaving this kindly band of men and their ordered life, and instinctively he felt that he would not return. At the edge of the forest he turned to take one last look at the huddle of huts, and saw a robed figure raise an arm in farewell at the gate. He waved his hand in reply, then turned his face towards the trees.

It was strange, walking with Owain again in the fresh chill of dawn, with the sun rising slowly to melt the frost-stiffened grass, and a light mist creeping up from the valley bottom. Caradoc had grown during the past months, but Owain had grown even more, seeming almost a man with his long striding legs, his deeper voice and large strong hands. As soon as they were away from the monks house and safely among the trees his uneasiness fell away, and his attitude to Caradoc became as it had ever been, patronizing, domineering and a little scornful.

Caradoc's mind seethed with questions.

"What happened - that Beltane day - afterwards?"

"After you got away? Oh, there was a fine to-do! They took a count of everyone, and when they found you were gone they all knew what had happened. Everyone remembered the hours you spent prattling to the prisoner. Brychan was mad enough to have struck you dead on the spot, never mind the Beltane fire!" He grinned at the memory. "It was sticky for a time, I can tell you! If Tiernan hadn't been chief I think I might have ended up a sacrifice myself, though they never suspected I'd helped you escape." He laughed, and swiped at a spider's web, sparkling with dewdrops, that stretched across their path. "We killed the best ewe-lamb for a sacrifice instead, but nearly everyone wished it had been the Roman."

"And did no one ever suspect where I was?"

"I think Brychan did. I think he'd have burnt out the monks, but Tiernan wouldn't agree to do it. I don't know why. I never told him you were there, but he might have guessed. Tiernan and Brychan were never much in agreement after that."

"How did Brychan die?"

"I see you're just the same, little brother - questions, questions and more questions!" said Owain mockingly. "I'll answer this once more, then I want peace. It's a long walk home, Father couldn't spare horses because they're wanted for hunting, and I want to save my breath. Brychan had a cut from a sharp stone, only a small cut but it festered and the poison spread. None of the cures seemed to work - some said it was another curse on the village. He died after ten days and, as I told you, Druce is Arch Druid in his place now."

Caradoc wanted badly to ask more about Islean, but decided it was better maybe not to annoy Owain. Anyway, the sooner they got to the village the sooner he would be able to see her for himself.

It was a long day, climbing steadily through the autumn woods, thick underfoot with dry, coloured fallen leaves that rustled as they walked. They drank from the stream, and ate the noon-piece that Brother John had hastily put up for them, and dusk was

beginning to fall again when at last they reached the
mouth of the pass.

Chapter 11

Caradoc had thought never to see his home again. The village, with its snarling, quarrelling dogs, its shrill women and children and rude huts seemed familiar yet somehow alien to him after the quiet routine he had become accustomed to. Above it all he smelt the acrid scent of wood-smoke, and caught a glimpse of white robes up near the grove and the sacred stones. He answered quickly the curious greetings that were called to him, and crossed the beaten ground quickly to the chieftain's hut.

Tiernan was there, having just eaten his meal and sent away the woman who tended Islean. Now he sat beside his mother's rough couch himself, ready to wake her and give her a cup of soup when it had cooled a little.

"Father!" Caradoc spoke the one word, standing just inside the doorway, and Tiernan sprang to his feet, almost spilling the soup. Caradoc saw that he seemed older, greyer than he remembered, and that there were deep new lines furrowing his face. Next moment he found himself clasped in strong arms, then released as suddenly.

"Son! I had doubts that your brother would find you! Or even that you still lived - "

Caradoc felt a lump in his throat. He had never known his father embrace him before, or even touch him except for a cuff in punishment or a slap across the shoulders when he had done well. He swallowed, and said "I am alive, and well, father. I trust that your own health is good."

From the doorway behind him, Owain laughed mockingly. "A pretty speech!"

Tiernan took no notice. "I am well. But your grandmother - "

They both looked down at Islean upon the bed. Her skin looked feverish and dry, and even in sleep her lips moved restlessly, her fingers plucking at the covers. She seemed somehow shrunken too, and much older. Caradoc touched her cheek and felt its burning heat.

"She has been like this for six days now," said Tiernan in a low voice. "And all the last three, calling for you. I fear she will not live, but it will comfort her to see you beside her if she wakes again." He straightened up. "I will see to my dogs and horses. Come Owain."

He turned and strode out, followed by Owain, who had found a cold shoulder of mutton and was holding it in his hand taking bites from it. Caradoc was hungry again, too, but he sat down beside Islean's bed so that she would see him the moment she awoke. After a while she stirred a little and her eyelids flickered. Caradoc leaned forward. "Islean?"

She opened her eyes and looked at him, but at first did not seem to recognise him. "Islean - grandmother - it's Caradoc!"

"Caradoc!" Her voice was weak, but it held a note of gladness. She struggled to rise, but the effort was too much. Caradoc picked up the soup.

"Let me give you some of this, Islean." She feebly waved the soup away. "No, no. Not yet. Just let me look at you."

Her eyes were feverishly bright as she looked hungrily at him, noticing his growth, the healthy tan to his cheeks and his trimmed hair. Like Tiernan, she did not ask where he had been, but her next words showed that she knew quite well.

"Caradoc, I believe - that I am dying. My life has been long enough. I am old - more than fifty summers - and you and Owain are grown now. But - " she paused and looked searchingly into his eyes. "But - but - I do not want to go like this, with the Druids chanting their spells, and the fear, and the darkness - "

She paused again, breathing hard, and Caradoc saw that there was indeed a look of fear in her eyes. "Is there another way, Caradoc?" she whispered.

Caradoc clutched both her hands in his. "Islean - yes! Yes, there is another way! You don't have to go out into the darkness in fear - "

And speaking clearly and earnestly, he began to tell her of the one he had learned to know at the monks house and in the words of Scripture, Jesus the Lord Christ who had lived on earth as a humble man and died on a Roman cross.

At the mention of the cross a light came into Islean's eyes.

"Then the dying man on the cross was this Lord Christ? And you say that he died for our sins? My heart

75

tells me that I have many sins in my own life. But why should the Lord Christ care for that?"

"Because he is the son of the one true God, who made us all and who loves us as his children," said Caradoc. "He died willingly, making himself a sacrifice and taking himself the punishment that should rightly be ours for our sins. Through faith in him we can go free, and after death go to be with him for ever in the next world."

Islean lay and listened with longing in her eyes. "All my life I have believed that there must be a better way than the ways we have known," she said quietly at last. "I have longed to find it almost from a child. Often I would go into the woods alone and cry out to the skies, asking for something - I knew not what - that would give me the inner peace I longed for. Can this be that better way, of which you speak? Can I believe too in this Lord Christ, Caradoc? Or is it too late for me, now that I am old and sick?"

"It's not too late," said Caradoc, and repeated the words with certainty. "It's not too late at all, Islean. You and I will pray to the Lord Christ, and ask him to receive you as one of his own."

"Quickly then, before someone comes!"

Caradoc had just finished his prayer, with Islean repeating the words after him, when there were foot-steps at the door. It was Tiernan, and with him Druce, the new Arch Druid.

"Druce has come to minister to you, Islean."

To everyone's surprise, Islean spoke out quite strongly. "I do not want him."

"But - you stand at death's door, Islean. You must

prepare yourself, and implore favour with the gods for the next life."

A hint of stubbornness had crept into Islean's voice. "Maybe I will not die after all. Maybe my strength will return. Anyway, if I do die I will go to the one true God, the Christian God. I have trusted in his son the Lord Christ and he has taken away my fear."

Tiernan looked thunderstruck, and Druce stared from Caradoc to the old woman on the bed and back again with a frown. Then he turned and departed without a word.

Looking at his grandmother, Caradoc was surprised to see that the angry fever flush had lessened and that there was a new look of peace in her eyes.

"Maybe I will not die after all," she repeated, and her lips smiled. "Maybe it is not yet my time. Anyway, I am hungry. Will someone give me that soup?"

Islean did not die. Instead, to the surprise of everyone, the fever receded and her strength began slowly to return. Within a day of Caradoc's homecoming she was sitting up and taking notice of her surroundings, in three more she was out of bed, sitting and giving directions to those about her.

Caradoc was overjoyed and spent many of those early autumn days with his grandmother, talking of his new life, about the monks and their teachings and the things he had learned from them. Islean listened hungrily to all he had to say, nodding her head from time to time. When she heard how new Christians were baptized after believing, following the example of the Lord Christ who had himself been baptized, she expressed a wish also to take this step in her new found faith. Caradoc was thoughtful for a while, wondering how it could be done without arousing the anger of the rest of the village and especially of the Druids. Then, one evening when everyone else seemed occupied about their own business, he fetched water in a cooking pot and himself baptized his grandmother in the name of the Father, the Son and the Holy Ghost.

Now that the crisis was past, Caradoc began to wonder again where his own future lay. No-one spoke of his leaving the village again. The Druids, though inclined to frown upon him in a disapproving way, seemed content to let the past lie and to accept again the returned son of their chieftain. After the first excitement everyone, including Tiernan and Owain, treated him exactly as before. He and Owain hunted and fished together, and the whole village made its preparations for the long winter ahead. Caradoc felt torn between returning to the quiet life with the monks, and staying with his family. He longed to continue with his reading and instruction, but there was Islean, who though recovered was old and frail, and who needed his help and support.

Then Tiernan, who had been restlessly occupied at home for several weeks, received word that a neighbouring tribe, just across the mountains, were planning a raid on the village. Almost with joy, Tiernan made preparations for a counter attack. This time, since Owain had grown and matured so much over the past months, it was decided that he should accompany his father.

It seemed strange to see Owain, who had stood so often gazing wistfully at the departing warriors, this time painting himself with the fearsome blue woad, preparing and honing his weapons and finally riding proudly off to battle beside his father, his head held high and the fierce light of conflict in his eye.

Caradoc sighed, watching them go. He knew that this time, as always, blood would be spilt and lives lost, women left without husbands and children fatherless, hearts broken and lives spoilt, and all for what? Because we have to prove that we are the bravest, and strongest, the most skilled and courageous in battle and afraid of no-one, Tiernan and Owain would have replied. He sighed again, thinking of the futility of it all. These aren't even Romans wishing to enslave us, these are just people like ourselves, only from another clan, he reasoned inside himself. Why cannot we all live peaceably together? But it was of no use to say these things. The fierce hill tribes only ever banded together in the face of a greater common enemy, and were sometimes too mistrustful to do so even then.

Islean was there at his elbow, heard the sigh and understood it. "Never mind. We have found the better way, you and I! Pray God that one day others here will find it too."

Caradoc's heart lifted. They would, if he had anything to say in the matter!

But he knew it would not be easy. From the corner of his eye he caught a glimpse of white robes as the Druids, up by the grove, also watched the departure of their warriors. Behind them, the sacred fire rose like incense to the vengeful gods.

It was only two days later that a sentinel, watching from the mouth of the pass, gave warning that the battle party was returning. Caradoc's heart missed a beat as he ran with others to catch the first sight. This time, there was no triumphant chanting, no singing - just a tired troop, bloodstained and weary, with dented shields and battered weapons, riding up the pass. They were led by Owain, his shaggy dark head bowed and his face sternly set with new grief. Behind him, carried by four spearmen, came the body of Tiernan.

Chapter 12

Tiernan's funeral took place with the full honours and ceremonies befitting a brave warrior and wise chieftain. A huge pyre of piled wood had been built at the edge of the stone circle, surrounded by dry kindling and brushwood. On this, clothed in the tribal garb of a Celtic chieftain and with his sword, shield and other weapons beside him, the body of Tiernan was placed. Heavy at heart, Caradoc watched as a warrior with a lighted torch approached the pyre, but turned unable to watch further as the torch was put to the kindling and the flames caught and began to lick upward. The chanting of the Druids began and was taken up by the assembled villagers, extolling the fierce virtues of their fallen chief, and imploring the gods for their favour in the after-realms. Owain stood among them, their new young chief, grieving yet proud of the way his father had died, and proudly conscious too of the fresh responsibility which now rested upon his young shoulders. Caradoc, in all the confusion of shock and change, knew only one thing clearly; that he had lost a father.

Above the voices of the people, the flames spread and crackled. Later, when the ceremony was over, the ashes scattered and people returning sombrely to their own huts, Islean took Caradoc's elbow. Her face, which had seemed younger and fuller since her recovery from her illness, looked old and shrunken again. Tiernan had been her only son. But all she said was, "Your brother will need you by his side, now."

"Yes."

The inauguration of a new chief required more ceremonies and invocations, which would spread over several days. Already Owain seemed aloof from the rest of them, no longer a boy, his forehead furrowed with new responsibility as he moved into his destined position in the village. Caradoc's heart ached for him, for Islean and for himself. His brother's new life would not be easy. For a time, at least, he himself must stay and offer his support and help. He felt it was what the Lord Christ would wish. Without being asked, he moved his brother's weapons and possessions into the sleeping-place that had been Tiernan's, establishing the new order of things.

On the morning after the funeral, Caradoc woke early when the first streaks of dawn were lightening the sky outside. On the chieftain's bed, Owain slept the heavy slumber of exhaustion, and Islean too, was asleep as he got up and quietly left the hut.

Only a dog or two opened an eye or thumped a tail at him as he walked through the chilly dawn to the mouth of the pass, the sense of loss heavy like a stone inside him. Away in the valley a blanket of fog lay like a fallen cloud, drifting and swirling a little, but above it the first rays of the sun began to shine from a cold but sunny sky. He guessed that, far below, the monks would by now have finished working down their ploughed land and planted their winter corn.

Caradoc passed Cynan, the sentry on duty, who raised a hand in sombre greeting as the boy appeared, and then stamped about a little, waving his arms to get the circulation going. Caradoc never envied the sentinels their duty, especially when the nights turned cold, the hours dragged and sleep pressed heavily upon the eyelids.

He said, "Go home, Cynan, and see about your breakfast. I'll watch for a bit."

Left alone, he looked again at the valley. Thick white fog, following the river, coming up almost to the edge of the forest, swirling and moving like a living thing.

He blinked and looked again. It was not just the fog that moved. Something was coming out of the fog, travelling upward into the clear air above. Many things. A line of men in breastplates that glittered in the first rays of early sun, short swords, and helmets from which eagles feathers waved.

Enemy invaders! Caradoc leapt from the earthwork in a single bound, a loud cry of warning on his lips. In a moment, all was confusion. Dogs barked, half-dressed men hurried from their homes, there was a clinking of hastily snatched spears and swords and shields. For a moment there was more confusion as some of the men, forgetting for the moment that their chief was dead, called for Tiernan and looked for him to direct them. But there was only Owain, rushing from the chief's hut, first bewildered and then determined, his father's sword in his hand.

By the time the Romans reached the pass the warriors had formed ranks of a kind, and were gathered to defend the mouth of the pass, others climbing the earthworks in order to hurl stones and other missiles onto the heads of the approaching enemy. It was not the first time they had been attacked by Romans, but Caradoc saw at once that this band of armed men was by far the biggest they had ever fought, well outnumbering their own men. Also, there was no Tiernan to lead the defence.

Nevertheless, it seemed for a while that they would hold the pass, and so thwart entry to the village, where the old women and small children had retreated to the shelter of the sacred grove and the protection of the Druids. The younger women, with the older children and old men, took their places on the earthworks, ready to hurl down spears, boulders and whatever else came to hand.

Caradoc, somewhere in the middle of it all with a shield and sword in his hands, was conscious of nothing but the need to defend his home and people, an instinct bred in him for generations. He hacked at an arm holding a Roman sword, and lifted his shield to parry a thrust from a Roman spear. Men were falling around him, their own and the enemy. There was a fearful clamour of battle in the air and a smell of blood and sweat. In spite of everything, Caradoc was conscious of the order and discipline of the Roman soldiers, and for a moment the thought of Lucius flashed through his mind. Up ahead of him, Owain hacked and slashed. His chance to prove himself had come sooner than he had expected, and

Caradoc knew that Owain would have had it no other way.

A Roman face, topped by a plumed helmet, loomed suddenly above him, looking down with what seemed to be a sneer into the boy's face, and a Roman arm was raised high to strike. Caradoc raised his shield to protect himself, but was a split second too late. A crushing blow from the flat of a sword descended on his head, sparks flew before his eyes and the clamour of battle died in his ears.

Chapter 13

Caradoc did not know how long it was before his senses returned to him. He was half-aware of a bumping, jarring journey where he partly awoke, dizzy and sick, to quickly lapse into unconsciousness again. When his head cleared enough for his eyes to open and his mind register what had happened, he found himself lying on a rough bed in some strange building.

A man's voice spoke. "Aha! The young cub's eyes flicker at last!" and another replied, "he has been senseless for a long time. I fear the blow may have permanently damaged his brain, though he is otherwise unmarked."

"I think not. These barbarians have thick skulls. See, he raises his head. Get him a drink. When he is fully recovered he should fetch a good price at Glevum."

Caradoc found that his head throbbed when he moved it, and that he was weak and dizzy still. A cup of water was held to his lips and he drank thirstily from it. He blinked hard to focus his blurred vision, and when it cleared saw that the cup was held by a Roman, hawk-faced and grinning not unkindly.

"That's right, youngster. Drink again, and I'll get something for you to eat. The market is but two days away, and I want you on your feet and looking lively by then."

Caradoc did not know what he meant. He stared wildly about him and tried to rise, but fell back again, sick and dizzy.

"Easy, easy," said the Roman. "Give yourself time. You almost had your skull cracked open."

Caradoc wanted to ask about his brother and the rest of his people, but the man was striding away from him and leaving the room, which was small and bare, like a clean cell. When Caradoc staggered shakily to his feet and tried the door, he found it secured, and the only window was little more than a slit. He was a prisoner, something so foreign to his free nature that for a moment a sense of panic overtook him. For a while he paced the floor like a caged animal, then sank down again on the bed with his head in his hands.

Food was brought but he could scarcely touch it, to the annoyance of his Roman captors. All his garbled questions and enquiries were greeted with indifferent shrugs and shakes of the head. It seemed that no-one knew anything of his people, or cared less.

Next day Caradoc, hands tied behind his back, was marched out of the room and into the cold drizzle of a November noon, through streets with bewildering noises and dwellings packed close, and into a large open space in the middle of the town. The man in charge of him was in a bad mood, cursing alike the miserable British weather, the shortage of wealthy buyers and the dejected looks of Caradoc.

"Hold yourself up, boy, and show what you're made of! Throw your chest out a bit. Let 'em see your muscles, but take that murderous sullen look off your face!"

He gave him a fierce prod in the small of the back with the stick he carried.

A sad collection of humanity was lined up under an awning in the market place, damp and bedraggled, waiting to be sold as slaves. Some were elderly people, a white-haired grandmother as old as Islean, an old man with toothless gums and watery, fearful eyes. They were sold off very cheaply, for all could see not much work was left in them.

There was fierce bidding for the younger ones, especially those whose sellers claimed were specially trained in some way, in making pastry or tending fruit trees, in dairying or needlework. Also in demand were the children, some as young as six or seven and born into slavery, who could be trained and moulded to serve their captors in whatever way was desired.

Caradoc kept his eyes downcast as one after another stepped up to the platform, stood bound while bids darted back and forth, and were led away by the highest bidder. All of them were strangers to him, and he took a small comfort from the knowledge that, by all appearances, he was the only one of his people to suffer this humiliation.

A prod in the back from the slave-master told him that it was his turn, but he kept his eyes resolutely downcast. He heard the man's voice intoning "This is a young barbarian, twelve or thirteen years old, fresh from the hills of the Welsh borderland. He is unbroken, but could have many possibilities - a sportsman or a horseman, maybe. With his knowledge of sword and spear he has potential as a gladiator. His muscles are hard, he is swift of foot and keen of eye."

"That we cannot judge for ourselves, for he keeps his head bowed to his chest," said a voice near Caradoc. "Raise your head, fellow!"

Caradoc would have kept his head down, but another sharp prod from the slave-master, accompanied by a sharp tug to the back of his hair, jerked it up in spite of himself. The pain brought tears to his eyes, but he blinked them back and stared defiantly at the collection of Roman buyers before him. Middle-aged and older men for the most part, retired soldiers now settled on holdings granted them by the Emperor, their faces swam before him.

A fattish, double-chinned man stepped forward and pinched Caradoc's biceps. "Hmm. Good and hard. Are you strong, boy?"

He spoke in the Roman language and Caradoc stared, not fully understanding. The man had small, deep-set eyes with a hint of cruelty in their depths. Pig's eyes, thought Caradoc dully.

"Insolent, at any rate," remarked the man, and sharply tweaked the boy's left ear. "Answer, boy. Or are you deaf and dumb too?"

Another man stepped forward, tall and upright, in the tunic and cloak of a Roman countryman. "Stay, Terentius! He doesn't understand you."

He went on, speaking in Caradoc's own tongue, "How are you called?"

Caradoc found himself staring into keen dark eyes in a weathered face. He had almost decided to keep up a stubborn refusal to reply, but something in the searching glance of the man held his own gaze, so that they remained for a moment eye to eye.

Then he said in a low voice, "Caradoc, son of Tiernan."

"And your age?"

"Thirteen summers."

"You are strong?"

"Yes."

"And can manage horses?"

"Yes."

"Hmm." The tall Roman considered for a moment, rubbing his chin, then stepped back. "Very well. Let the bidding commence."

The bids for the boy flew thick and fast across the market place. More than one wealthy Roman liked the looks of the sturdy young Celt with the proud bearing and the handsome features. He lowered his head again in humiliation, sending up a silent prayer to the Lord Christ, who had once stood as helpless as himself and must surely understand his feelings.

"Twenty one sestertiums!" was the last sum called and the bidding was over.

"Sold, to Julius Terentius!"

Caradoc felt the slave-master's stick prodding him to get down from the platform. He did so, and found himself the newly-acquired property of the fat man with the double chin and piggy eyes.

Chapter 14

Caradoc's heart sank to a new depth as he stumbled from the platform and allowed himself to be led away. The fat man seemed pleased with his purchase, smiling smugly and urging along his new slave with a sly tweak here and a painful pinch there, confirming the promise of subtle cruelty that Caradoc had seen in his small eyes. Somehow this was far worse than the straightforward buffetings and rough handling he had endured so far. Again he thought of the Lord Christ, of the humiliation and scorn and spitting he had suffered at Roman hands before his cruel crucifixion. Deep inside himself he cried a silent prayer of agony. 'Oh, Lord Christ! I'd rather die than go with this man! Have mercy on me!'

At the edge of the market-place Julius Terentius and his slaves came to a halt. Standing with lowered head, Caradoc was aware of an exchange of words between his new master and someone else, growing more heated by the moment, while the crowd surged and murmured around them.

"You had your fair chance in the market!" Terentius

was saying, his voice loud and belligerent. "If you weren't such a tight-fisted old miser, Justus Pollus, you could easily have outbid me. Well, I bought him fair and square and I'm hanging on to him!"

Caradoc raised his head to see the tall dark Roman farmer standing and talking to Terentius. The tall man frowned and half turned away. Then, seeing the boy's eyes upon him, he seemed to change his mind and turned back again, spreading his hands in a gesture of asking.

"Five sestertiums extra, then."

Terentius laughed, his double chins wobbling with amusement.

"My, my! I never thought I'd see the day! This pup must really have taken your fancy, Justus, to make you so eager to part with your money! Well, maybe I'm not that pleased with him myself after all. He looks a sullen enough cur! Tell you what, you throw in a couple of fat lambs and he's yours!"

The bargain was struck and the fat man moved off, chuckling.

Caradoc felt a sense of relief. He opened his mouth to thank the other Roman, but only choked a little. The tall farmer was looking at him rather grimly.

"Hold your head up, boy, and look a bit lively. I hope you spoke the truth when you said you were a good horseman?"

Caradoc gulped and nodded.

"Good. You'll need to be, to give me some return for such an outlay of money. I'm not used to paying so much for my slaves, I can tell you! But, knowing Terentius of old, I hadn't the heart to let you go with him. Come on, then. Move your bones. We'll get straight home and see what stuff you're made of."

He turned with a swirl of his warm homespun cloak and strode off. Caradoc followed. There was nothing else he could do. And for the moment his strongest feeling was still one of relief, even though he was now a slave to the Roman.

The villa of Justus Pollus, on the outskirts of the town of Glevum, was the most magnificent building Caradoc could ever have imagined, even seen through a thin cold drizzle of November rain. It stood just off the road, surrounded by cornfields with the stubble ploughed in ready for next years crops. Before it was a beautifully laid-out garden, surrounded by an elegant marble balustrade, and graceful pillars flanked the imposing front door. All this Caradoc glimpsed before he was taken by an older slave round the side of the house and into the slaves' quarters at the back.

He was given his own sleeping-room, another cell-like space but clean and neat, with walls of whitewashed stone. Here he was brought a meal, thick curd soup of black beans, wheaten bread and goats cheese, and told to sleep as much as he wished until the morning, when his new duties would begin.

Still weak and a little shaken from his recent concussion, Caradoc was glad to lie quietly on the narrow bed. Sobs rose in his throat as he thought of all he had lost. He was exiled for the second time in his life, and this time he feared that there would be no return.

"Oh Lord Christ, grant me your strength to bear this, if bear it I must!" he prayed, feeling the tears wet on his cheeks. He had heard muttered mention of suicide among some of the other slaves sold that day, and for a moment the thought hovered in his own mind. But he knew that this was not the way for a follower of the Lord Christ.

Early next morning Caradoc was woken by a sharp-faced young man, five or six years older than himself, who flung a suit of woven cloth beside the bed.

"Put those on," he ordered, giving a look of scorn at Caradoc's discarded clothing of sheepskin and leather. "Then come to the quarters for your breakfast." He hesitated at the doorway, then turned to speak again. "By the way, I'm Cassius and I'm in charge of the stables here. You'll be taking orders from me."

Caradoc noticed the superiority in the voice of the other boy, but said nothing. He waited for Cassius to leave.

But Cassius continued, with a slight sneer "You haven't lived at a properly run farm before, I don't suppose?"

Caradoc wished that Cassius would go about his business.

"If you mean a Roman place, then, no, I haven't," he said as politely as he could.

"Thought not. You can always pick out a barbarian. What's it like, living up in the hills like a savage?"

Caradoc felt his temper begin to rise. There was a time when he would have smashed his fist into the other boy's sneering face, and for a moment his knuckles ached to do just that. But he knew that this kind of reaction would not have been pleasing to the Lord Christ, who had himself borne cruel scorn and mockery with never a word.

He said evenly "It was good. Free."

A lump came into his throat and he turned his head away.

But Cassius only said scornfully, "Huh - freedom! I don't suppose it's all it's cracked up to be!" He waited for a reply, but, receiving none, walked off with a jaunty step. Staring after him, Caradoc realised with a strange shock that the older boy had never known what it was to be free. A hint of pity stirred somewhere deep inside him.

In the course of the first day he found himself the object of curiosity, scorn, and even derision from most of the other slaves. Most of them had been in captivity for years. Many, like Cassius, had been slaves since early childhood. The appearance of a young barbarian in their midst was something new.

Caradoc spent the morning being instructed by Cassius in the layout of the stables, the number and status of the horses, their care and management and that of their harness and equipment. He was then told to clean out the stables.

"Can you ride?" asked Cassius.

Caradoc nodded, and was told to mount a bay horse and show what he could do. He trotted, cantered and galloped round the stable paddock, and came to a halt to the sound of applause. Justus Pollus himself stood at the paddock rail, smiling approval. "Well done! You are an able horseman! Do all your kinsmen ride?"

Caradoc nodded, dismounting. "Yes. We start as babies, almost."

"I can see you are experienced. It will be to your advantage. Now, after you have had your noon meal, come into the atrium to meet my wife. My wife always speaks with all new slaves."

He strode away. From the stable doorway, Cassius flung a resentful glance at the younger boy. "Making ourselves popular, are we?"

Caradoc didn't reply. That seemed to be the best way of dealing with Cassius.

After the noon meal, having made himself clean and neat as instructed, he presented himself where he had been directed, at the large hall in the centre of the building from which most of the other rooms opened. This atrium was a most beautiful place, with graceful pillars soaring from a marbled floor to lofty ceilings, a sparkling fountain splashing into a pool in the middle of the room, and around the pool a profusion of exotic plants. Among the plants sat a lady, approaching middle-age but with the most beautiful face and serene expression Caradoc had ever seen.

She smiled at the boy standing awkwardly before her. "Sit down," she said, indicating a low footstool at her feet. When he had done so she went on, in a low sweet voice. "So you are the young Celt from the hills of Wales! Tell me about your family. Have you a father, mother, brothers, sisters?"

Caradoc stared at her and suddenly his eyes blurred with tears. He gulped and said, "I - I don't know. That is - no father and mother. My mother died when I was a baby and - and - my father's funeral was just the day before I was captured. I have a brother and a grand-mother, but - but - "

And suddenly, to his own dismay and chagrin, he found himself blubbering like a baby before the sympathy in her eyes, and pleading incoherently, "Oh, please, lady - please, can you ask about them for me? Can you tell me whether they still live "

"My poor boy!" The lady's eyes were a little moist also. "There - don't cry so. I understand - I am a mother myself. You have been through much. Yes, I will enquire for you. But I can promise nothing."

She waited a little while he recovered himself, drawing the back of his hand across his tear-stained face.

"My husband is a just man. You will not be badly treated here, if you do your best. Tell me, have you ever heard of the Lord Jesus Christ?"

The sudden question made Caradoc stiffen to an upright position upon the stool. He stared at the lady. "Why - yes. I - I am a follower of the Lord Christ myself."

The lady clasped her hands in joy. "You are a Christian? Oh, how wonderful!" She suddenly laughed merrily. "My husband accuses me of trying to convert all our new slaves to Christianity, but I see that with you I will have my trouble spared! Tell me, how did it come about?"

Caradoc felt his spirits rise as he told the lady of his visit to the monks house and subsequent stay there. She listened eagerly, eyes sparkling, hands clasped together. When he had finished she laughed again and said, "So our faith is spreading like a flame across the land, even into the remote valleys and hills! May God be praised! And can you read the scriptures for yourself, Caradoc?"

"I was learning," said Caradoc, and the lady said quietly, "then you shall learn more. Every seventh day I gather together those of our people who will listen, and read and teach them the words of the Lord Christ. Some of them, I am afraid, are not sincere, but I trust that the seed sown will yet find some good ground. My husband, alas, is still a follower of Mithras, but I pray for him daily. You shall join us at our studies. Will that please and cheer you?"

Caradoc already felt extraordinarily cheered. It seemed something like a miracle to him to find followers of the Lord Christ here, among the Romans.

"And will you explain things I don't understand?"

"Of course, if I am able. Now go, back to your duties, in case my husband grows impatient. And may God go with you."

Chapter 15

"Hurry up there!" said Cassius loudly, flicking a riding whip impatiently against his boot. "That stretch of fence should be finished by now. Our master's fine new stallion could arrive at any time."

Caradoc raised his head, with some resentment, from hammering the last nail into place. "I'm going as fast as I can."

Cassius leaned forward to push his face close to Caradoc's. "Well, I say it's not fast enough."

Caradoc was stung into a quick retort. "What you say doesn't matter. You're only a slave the same as me!"

Cassius raised the whip, and for a moment Caradoc thought that it was going to come down upon his head. Then the older boy's anger seemed to collapse into a kind of despair, and his arm dropped. He said, almost wistfully, "I'll be free one day, you'll see. What's it like, really?"

Caradoc's annoyance melted in a rush of pity. It was not the first time the older boy had questioned him about his former life. Sometimes, when Cassius forgot to be his usual bullying, sneering self, he showed a pathetic eagerness to hear of the life Caradoc had lived before.

It was a raw day in early December, and the breaths of the two slaves hung like thick fog in the frosty air. They had been ordered to raise the height of the paddock fence by two rails, to accommodate an expensive and mettlesome new horse purchased by Justus Pollus, and had worked at it for the past few days. To-day Justus Pollus was occupied with a visitor, and they worked alone.

Caradoc said slowly, "I've told you, it's good. To be able to gallop through the woods until you're tired, to spear wild pig and shoot deer, to hear the wind roar in the treetops when you're sitting by the fire polishing your own spear on a winter night - " He stopped suddenly, almost overcome by the memories. Cassius too, had a faraway look in his eyes as though he too, sensed the freedom.

But next moment his mood had changed abruptly, his eyes narrowed and he pointed with the riding whip. "Get on with the job! You'll have to take the last rail off and nail it again. It's crooked! It might do for rough barbarians but it won't do for civilized folk."

To give his words emphasis, he gave Caradoc a jab in the ribs with the handle of the riding whip. Caradoc's pity melted as quickly as it had come. Suddenly he could no longer stand the other boy's moods and insults, his sneers and bullying. How dared Cassius stand there giving orders like a lord and brandishing the whip! Ignoring the little warning voice in his mind, he whirled with a loose piece of railing still in his hand, raised it high and knocked the whip from the other boy's hand.

After the first moment of shock, the face of Cassius became contorted with rage. He snatched up another length of rail and lunged at Caradoc, aiming a vicious swipe at the younger boy's head. Caradoc parried the blow with his own weapon, and tried to knock the rail from his opponents hand. Breathing hard, they faced each other, lunging and thrusting, their frustrations and differences finding expression. Cassius was several years older than Caradoc, strong and toughened by years of stable work, but Caradoc had the advantage of a quick mind and a hard, nimble body. Each had received minor buffets from the weapon of the other, and Cassius, almost beside himself with rage, was gathering himself for a crushing blow to Caradoc's skull when the other boy quickly dived low and neatly tripped Cassius with a whack across the shins. Carried forward by the impetus of his own blow, Cassius found himself sprawling on the muddy ground.

"Bravo!" The sound of laughter and applause sounded from the paddock rail, where Justus Pollus and another man, a dark-faced Roman, obviously his visitor, had watched the affair. Cassius scrambled to his feet, scowling murderously, while Caradoc stood with the length of railing still in his hand, breathing hard and suddenly very much ashamed of his outburst of temper. The laughter and applause came from the dark-faced man, who had clearly enjoyed the spectacle of two young slaves setting about each other with a will. Justus Pollus, however, did not seem to share his visitor's amusement. With a stern face he ordered both boys back to their work, with threats of punishment for any further fighting.

"And you - " he pointed unsmilingly at Caradoc, "you report to my lady in the atrium when you have finished work and tidied yourself."

The two Romans turned and strolled together towards the villa, leaving the boys to gather themselves together.

"I'll get you for this!" muttered Cassius as he took himself off to change his muddy clothing.

As he later washed and changed himself in order to obey the summons of the lady Helena, Caradoc felt a twinge of apprehension. Was he to be reprimanded for his share in the morning's events? He did not wish to distress the lady, who had been kindness itself to him on the occasions when, together with any other slaves who wished, they had met together to share instruction in the Christian faith and the teaching of Scriptures. Justus Pollus too was a fair if strict master, himself overseeing the work that Caradoc did, the cleaning of the stables, the feeding and watering of the horses in the early morning, and later in the day the exercising of the same fine horses. The routine, though long and hard, was not altogether unpleasant, had it not been for the constant ache of homesickness and longing for the freedom of his old life.

Presenting himself at the door of the atrium, Caradoc had the sudden wild hope that the lady had the news of his family that he longed for. But one glance at her face showed him that the news, if any, was not favourable.

"I have made enquiries about your people as you asked," she began, looking at him with compassion as he stood expectantly before her. "And I have spoken to one who was at the battle where you were taken. But I'm afraid the news is not good. There were many losses, among our men as well as your people. But we did not take the village, it seems. Our men finally retreated, but I do not know in what condition your people were left, or how many survived, or how they have fared since then."

"This man - did he know anything of my brother?" asked Caradoc eagerly.

"He thinks that a young chieftain was struck down, sorely wounded and bleeding, but whether he lived or died he could not tell. You were the only prisoner taken, except for two wounded who died soon after. I'm sorry, Caradoc. The man could tell me no more than that."

"Thank you my lady." Caradoc turned to go, his heart heavy. He did not think it likely that Owain had survived. As to the rest of the village, it sounded as though it had been left in sorry straits, with many of the warriors killed or maimed. What would happen now to the women and children, to the old men and women, to Islean if she still lived? How would they defend themselves, hunt for food, strengthen the huts against the cold and survive the coming winter?

He turned back impulsively. "My lady. Oh, my lady - is there no way I could be released and return to my people? They need me - who will care for them this winter? Please, please, could your husband not let me go?" She shook her head sadly. "No, Caradoc, he would never do that, even for me. He paid a good sum for you, and my husband is a man who likes value for money. You are doing well here, and he is pleased with you. In fact - "

She paused and then went on "Justus has told me that

this morning you fought with the slave Cassius?"

Caradoc flushed a little, fingering the sore and bruised places on his face.

"Yes, my lady."

"My husband and his friend saw the whole thing. Cassius has a mean and spiteful streak, though we must ever remember that he too is a human soul precious in the eyes of the Lord Christ, and to be valued as such. But the point is this. My husband's friend Drucus was most impressed by the skill you showed in striking and fending off blows. He has made an offer to Justus to buy you and have you trained as a gladiator. Be warned, Caradoc. I would advise you, at all costs, to make yourself so indispensable to my husband that he will not easily be persuaded to part with you."

She paused again, and went on hurriedly "You see, as a trained and skilful gladiator, you would go to Rome. You would appear at the Coliseum, before the Emperor; you would be forced to kill in the arena or be killed yourself. And - you are a Christian. There is sore persecution of Christians in Rome."

Caradoc stared at her. He knew that the Christians were often hated and feared, that houses of monks had been burned and the occupants murdered in their beds. But the only opposition he had received in this Roman household had been a little sneering and sarcasm from some of the other slaves, who accused him of toadying to his captors.

The lady Helena's cheeks were a little pale. "You do not know what happens, maybe. Here in this land we have much freedom to worship as we will. But I have also lived in Rome. I have seen. The Emperor hates

Christians. It is sport to him to have them burned alive, torn to pieces by lions or wild bulls, or forced to kill one another in the arena with sword and cestus."

She trembled a little. Caradoc thought of the dark-faced man Drucus who had so keenly applauded him that morning, and said "I will try to avoid the man, my lady, for your sake. I have no wish to go to Rome. I wish only to return to my own village."

Helena sighed. "And I fear that is impossible. Go carefully now, Caradoc. I will pray for you."

Chapter 16

There was no happier horse owner in the land than Justus Pollus on the day that his new stallion was delivered to his farm by the horse dealer. A thin wintry sunshine had broken through grey clouds, making the jet black coat of the horse gleam like a rook's wing as he was led into the paddock.

The name of the horse was Dominus. "And could there be a more suitable name?" asked Justus Pollus of the world in general. "Did anyone ever see more lordly a creature? Is he not truly magnificent?"

The entire household, slaves included, had gathered to watch the new arrival. Dominus was indeed a splendid animal, seventeen hands high at the shoulders, muscles rippling under the shining well-groomed coat, hooves dancing with restless energy and proud head tossing against the halter as he was led by the dealer, a swarthy, shrewd-eyed man.

"Loose him and let us see the looks of him when he is without restraint," ordered Justus Pollus.

Caradoc saw that the man made rather hastily for the

paddock rail as soon as he had taken the halter from the horse's head. Everyone else had eyes only for Dominus, who as soon as he felt himself freed gave a great whinnying plunge, then reared up on his strong hind legs and was off galloping like the wind across the paddock, wheeling at the fence to gallop back and then racing round and round inside the fence with clods of earth flying up from his churning hooves. Everyone moved back a little from the newly-reinforced fence.

"By Jupiter, it's a good thing we added those two extra rails to the height!" murmured Justus, rubbing his chin. "The brute looks as though he could easily clear anything an inch or two lower. How he gallops! He has hardly slackened speed at all!"

"He is completely tireless," said the horse-dealer at his elbow. "Truly a lord among horses. And in the peak of condition, as you can see."

Everyone watched in respectful silence as the black horse continued its gallop, hooves thudding and long tail streaming behind.

"Bring a saddle," ordered Justus Pollus at last. "I would like to see the animal put through its paces. You mount first, fellow, and let us see what he can do."

But, strangely, the horse-dealer had seemed to melt away and disappear in the last few minutes. "Confound the fellow!" said Justus irritably. "These dealers are as slippery as mercury! Never mind, the deal is completed. Saddle and bridle the brute and I will ride him myself."

It took four slaves, running and dodging to avoid the flying hooves, to corner the stallion and slip the bridle over his head. He waited, nervous and quivering, eyes rolling a little and breath coming in quick snorts while the saddle was strapped into place. When Justus Pollus mounted from the rail, Dominus gave a loud snort of indignation, reared high with a squeal and began to buck and plunge. Justus, with his years of soldiering experience behind him, hung on for several moments before being flung from the saddle into the mud. The slaves, terrified, had loosed the horse's head and scattered in all directions.

The lady Helena, pale and frightened, hurried to the gate as her husband, nursing a wrenched wrist and cursing under his breath but otherwise uninjured, picked himself up and limped towards her. Across the paddock Dominus was galloping free again, the reins dangling.

"Justus, are you hurt?"

"Confound it, no! Not much, anyway. Why did those fools let go before I was ready? Look at him now, likely to trip over those reins and break a leg! Go after him, you idiots, don't just stand there! By Jupiter, Helena, but he is the most magnificent creature I've ever owned! Not properly broken though - that dealer fellow deceived me there! But we'll soon remedy that!"

"Not with an injured wrist. Come inside and let me bind it."

He allowed himself to be led away, muttering irritably but rather more shaken than he would admit. He was not as young as he had been, and the horse was stronger and more powerful than any he had ridden for a long time.

One after another the most experienced riders among the slaves tried to master Dominus, but one by one they took their turn at tumbling into the mud as he unseated them. At the end of the afternoon he was caught and led, trembling, but far from tired out, into his new stable quarters.

"You can rub him down and curry comb him," said Cassius sourly as they put fresh fodder in the manger. "I have no liking for the brute at all. He has a demon in him, that's what I reckon."

Cassius was one who had been thrown, and he was limping heavily from a bruised ankle. The black stallion jumped as he slammed the stable door crossly behind him. Caradoc spoke soothingly. "All right, all right. Quietly now, quietly! I know you don't like to be shut up. I feel the same. But we can't help it, either one of us."

He half expected Dominus to lash out with his hooves as he laid his hand upon the sweating black neck, and made ready to clamber over into the feeding passage if he needed to escape. But apart from a slight quivering, the black horse stood still. Still talking soothingly, Caradoc remembered a trick he had been taught when breaking the wild hill ponies back at home. Moving gently to the horse's head, he took the velvety nose between his hands and breathed gently into the flaring nostrils. Dominus tried at first to fling back his head, but gradually relaxed. Still keeping up the soothing flow of talk, Caradoc took up the brush and began to rub down the black coat streaked with drying sweat. By the time he had covered the first shoulder and was working down towards the fetlock, Dominus had lowered his head and was calmly eating his supper of oats.

Next day Justus Pollus, his injured wrist firmly strapped but his spirit indomitable, was again at the paddock when the new stallion was led out for his afternoon exercise. His eyes gleamed admiringly as he watched the pounding hooves and flying black mane and tail.

"What a creature! And here I am trussed up like a dressed fowl and unable to set foot in the stirrup!" His eyes swept the slaves who had accompanied him. "How about you fellows? Is any of you willing and ready to try again to mount him?"

"I cannot, master," said Cassius sullenly. He showed his bruised and swollen ankle. The other slaves shuffled their feet and averted their eyes. If their master ordered them to attempt to mount the horse they would have to obey. It was their fervent hope that he would not.

"Well, you are a sorry crowd!" said Justus Pollus in disgust. "You should count it a privilege to be on the back of such a magnificent animal. Even if it is only for a second or two!"

He smiled at his own joke, and one or two slaves sniggered uneasily. Caradoc plucked at the sleeve of his master's uninjured wrist.

"Sir, I will ride Dominus."

Someone sniggered again, a little louder. Justus Pollus looked down at the boy in astonishment. "You? Why, you are no more than a child! It needs a grown man to attempt to handle an animal of that mettle! You'd be off on your head in no time, and very likely crack your skull. And that would be a waste of the money I paid for you, would it not?"

"I think I could do it," said Caradoc. "I used to help break ponies with my father and the other warriors, and some of them were as wild as Dominus, though not as large. I'd like to try. Please."

Justus looked down at him for a long moment, considering. He said at last. "I see you are in earnest. Very well then, you shall try. But if you survive the first tumble you had better leave it at that."

Caradoc nodded. He waited while Dominus was caught and saddled, and approached the trembling horse as he stood by the paddock rail held by a slave. Reaching up, he took the horse's head between his hands and again breathed deep into his nostrils, talking quietly in a low crooning voice. Then he climbed the rail and flung a leg across the saddle.

The horse snorted a little and began its bucking and plunging routine as soon as its head was loosed. Caradoc talked soothingly into the wildly-pricked ears, gripping tight with his knees. Then instead of rearing, the horse broke into its accustomed gallop, but did not try further to unseat its rider. Round and round the paddock it raced, with Caradoc holding firmly to the reins. After the first few breathless moments he felt only exhilaration, the rushing of cold air past his face and the rhythm of the strong muscular body beneath him giving him the first feeling of real freedom he had experienced for a long time. Round and round they galloped, the turf flying from beneath the hooves of Dominus and his own spirits lifting by the minute.

"Bravo!" There was an exclamation from Justus, and a ripple of applause from those watching at the gate. Caradoc raised one hand in salute, enjoying himself. The next time round he caught the expression on the face of Cassius, a sullen jealous resentment at the success of the younger boy. But he did not see, nor did anyone else, the swift spiteful movement that Cassius made with the riding whip he held, sending the whip out across the hindlegs of Dominus as he pounded past.

Dominus had never before known the touch of a whip. At the sharp stinging pain he squealed shrilly and reared, all but unseating his young rider. Then, before Caradoc could quite recover his firm grip on the reins, the black stallion had seized the bit between his teeth and galloped full tilt across the paddock. Caradoc saw the high rail rushing to meet them, and knew that the horse was not going to swerve aside as he reached it. Frantically he tried to regain control of the bit, but it was too late. As they reached the railing, Dominus rose suddenly and soared into the air, clearing the rail by inches and landing safely on the other side. Next moment they were galloping across the pasture land on the other side, with the faint cries of the onlookers fading into the distance behind them.

Chapter 17

Pounding across the rich rolling farmland around Glevum, Caradoc realised that he had no choice but to give Dominus his head, at least until the horse began to tire. On they galloped, over pasture and meadow and rich dark soil ploughed for next year's crops, with Dominus sailing like a bird over hedges and ditches as they approached them. The breath of the great horse came in rapid snorts, his powerful muscles strained rhythmically under the smooth black coat, and Caradoc crouched low in the saddle as the winter landscape flashed by. It seemed that their rapid pace would never slacken.

At last, however, the boy became aware that the galloping hooves were gradually slowing and changing rhythm to a canter, and by the time the canter became a trot, he had regained control of the reins and was able to bring the horse to a halt.

Dominus lowered his head and his breath came in great shuddering gasps. Caradoc, panting too, twisted in the saddle and looked back the way they had come. They had covered many miles in their wild flight, leaving far behind them the villa and farm of Justus Pollus on the outskirts of the Roman town of Glevum. All around them spread the English countryside, a rolling patchwork of bare winter grassland, brown stubble and ploughed fields, with low buildings and thin plumes of smoke showing where small farmsteads lay in the gentle folds of the hills.

Turning again, Caradoc's heart seemed to miss a beat. Up ahead of him, dark grey and stark against the pale winter sky, lay the range of mountains marking the borderlands among which he knew his own village lay. Often, exercising the other horses in the afternoons, he had looked longingly at those distant hills, and once or twice had in his frustration and homesickness, thought of galloping away towards them. But he knew that this would be hopeless. The slaves were carefully watched at all times, and most of them were willing and ready to report on one another. He would quickly have been pursued and overtaken, and the punishment for runaways was severe.

Now, however, the hills seemed suddenly much nearer. It was possible to make out the darker masses of forests on their sides, and on the tops the white powdering of the first of the winter's snow. He held his breath, clutching the saddle bow as the implications struck him. The wild flight of Dominus had given him a rare chance, a chance he would not resist. Already he had covered a good part of the distance between Glevum and his home. With a horse like Dominus there was none that could catch up with him. He would be a fool not to take advantage of the opportunity.

Slipping from the stallion's back, Caradoc led him

over to a small pond of rainwater near where they had come to a halt. The sweat-streaked sides of Dominus heaved as he got back his wind, and he drank thirstily from the pond. While he drank, Caradoc patted the hot and sweating neck, noticing the muddied and lathered sides of the horse. Dominus should have a good rub down before he rested for the night, or he might take a chill in the wintry weather. But that would have to wait. When he thought that Dominus had drunk enough, Caradoc scooped a handful of water to drink himself, then swung back into the saddle and turned the horse's head towards the distant hills.

They travelled on at a good pace through the short winter afternoon, keeping always to farm or grassland and avoiding the busy Roman roads or footpaths, until dusk began to fall and a slender crescent moon came out to give its faint light. There was more than a hint of frost in the air, and Caradoc knew that he would have to find some kind of shelter for the night for himself and the horse. Nightfall had come when at last they came to a small farm nestled in the hollow of the hills, where a twinkling yellow light at the farmhouse window showed that the occupants had finished their evening work and retired indoors for the night. A large haystack stood nearby, which boy and horse stealthily approached, the hoofbeats muffled by the muddy ground around it. Caradoc dismounted and led Dominus to the side of the stack furthest from the farmhouse, where he halted the horse. Dominus was tired out, but revived at sight and smell of the sweet hay, which he began to pull from the stack in mouthfuls. While he munched it, Caradoc dismounted and unsaddled the horse, then took another wisp of hay dangling from his mouth, and nuzzled gently at Caradoc's face.

Caradoc was hungry and thirsty too. He found clean water in a stone tank nearby, which he drank himself and led the horse to drink from too. While Dominus munched more hay, Caradoc discovered a clamp of turnips a little way away, covered with clods of earth against the frost, and dug with his hands to uncover one. It tasted cold and muddy, but was better than nothing. Taking what was left of it for the morning, he returned to the horse, made him as comfortable as possible with more good hay from the stack, and himself burrowed deep into the haystack for warmth. There, despite the scratchiness and cramped position, he was soon asleep from sheer exhaustion.

He awoke before dawn, chilly and bewildered by his surroundings, until he remembered what had happened. The black horse was fast asleep, stretched out and blowing softly through velvety nostrils. Caradoc knew that they would have to be on their way before the farm people awoke and began their morning work. He rolled into a sitting position, pulling bits of hay from his head and the neck of his tunic, and scratching the itchy places. Then he remembered that he had forgotton his prayers the night before, and sat for a moment with knees drawn up and arms clasped around them.

Immediately his thoughts turned towards the Lord Christ, his determination seemed undermined by a strange feeling of inner conflict. For the first time he felt doubts about the rightness of his action in escaping and returning home. An inner argument began. 'I do not belong to Justus Pollus, he told himself, bunching his hands into fists on his knees. I was taken forcibly from my people, sold into slavery, all against my will. I belong with my own people. They are in sore distress and need me among them, and I have a right to go to them.'

The other voice said, 'But what about the horse, Dominus? You have no right to take him. He does not belong to you. Justus Pollus is his owner. Taking him makes you no more than a common thief.'

'I did not take him. He bolted with me on his back. I did not plan to escape. I did not steal him.'

'But you did not take him back.'

'Why should I?'

'Because you belong to the Lord Christ, and have promised to obey his commands.' Caradoc put his head down upon his knees and wept. He could not give up this chance. But suddenly he remembered something he had read from the Scriptures with Brother John and also with the lady Helena, how Jesus the Lord Christ had gone willingly to the cross even though he could have called on twelve legions of angels to rescue him from his enemies. He had groaned and pleaded with God his father to be allowed to escape if possible from his cruel fate, yet nevertheless set his face to do what was needed for the salvation of mankind.

Caradoc felt the hot tears slide down between his fingers, and sobs shook his shoulders. Beside him, Dominus woke with a snort, blew to clear his nostrils and climbed to his feet, shaking himself and stretching his magnificent limbs. Dawn was beginning to streak the dark sky, and somewhere nearer the farmhouse a rooster crowed. They must be on their way. He saddled the horse and took him to drink, scooping a little water for himself in his cupped hands. The horse, rested and full of fresh energy, snorted and tossed his head, eager to be off as he swung himself into the saddle. Caradoc took one last long look at the snow-capped hills of the distant borderland before he turned the head of the black stallion back towards Glevum.

Chapter 18

It was almost dark when Caradoc reached the farm of
Justus Pollus and rode in through the gate to the stable
yard. A young slave appeared from an outhouse and
stared at the boy and horse with an expression of
amazement. He was joined by another, and both
approached curiously as Caradoc dismounted stiffly at
the stable door.

"It is you -you have returned?" asked the younger
one uncertainly.

Caradoc's every bone, sinew and muscle seemed to
ache with weariness.

"It is I, and I have returned," he said heavily.

The two slaves looked as though they expected to see
Caradoc accompanied by an armed Roman or captor of
some kind. Seeing no-one, their mystification deepened. "You came of your own free will?"

"Yes."

Suddenly Caradoc was too weary even to reply to
questions. He led the big horse into his own stall and
closed the door in the faces of his two curious fellow

slaves. Then he fetched oats and hay from the feeding passage to put in front of the horse and began to groom the lathered and dirty black coat.

It was only a moment, however, before Cassius appeared beside the other two, scowling in over the stable door with an expression of mixed disbelief and curiosity. "So - you are back! We hadn't thought to see you again, or the horse! There was a fine to-do yesterday when you made off! Everyone said you'd stolen the horse, and your freedom!"

Caradoc didn't reply. He wished Cassius would go away and leave him to his work. But the commotion had been heard from the villa, and Justus Pollus himself came striding across the cobbled yard, his hand still in bandaging and his face a study of surprise and puzzlement. He had never before known a runaway slave to return of his own accord, and could scarcely believe it had happened. He was silent for a moment, peering in at the tired munching horse and the weary boy attending to its needs, and then said sternly, "When you've finished that, come out here."

By the time Dominus was groomed, fed, watered and bedded down with clean straw, Caradoc was so weary that he could barely stand. He closed the door behind him and faced Justus Pollus in the stable yard.

"Explain!" The Roman's lips were pressed into a hard tight line.

Caradoc gathered together his weary senses. "The horse bolted with the bit between his teeth - I don't know why. We had covered much ground before I could bring him to a halt. Then - I saw that I was far from here, and much nearer to my home. I decided I would ride on and return to my own people."

Justus drew in his breath sharply. "With my horse?"

Caradoc nodded. "At first I thought I would be justified in this, since I was captured and sold into slavery myself. Then - I remembered the command of Christ that we must not steal. This morning I decided to bring the horse back."

"And where did you spend the night, you and the horse?"

"Under a haystack at a farm. I fed and watered the horse, rubbed him down as best I could and bedded him with hay."

"Hm. I must examine him for myself."

He entered the stall and approached the munching Dominus, smoothing the black coat and running a hand down the stallion's limbs. Caradoc felt himself sway with weariness and leaned against the wall of the stable for support. When Justus Pollus emerged he peered keenly at the boy.

"The horse is well, and sound in wind and limb. I see that you have cared for him above your own needs. I believe that you are telling me the truth. I saw the horse bolt and knew that he was out of your control. I did not expect to see you or he again, though we mounted a search. It is a great relief that you have returned. Also the horse seems much quieter and more manageable. Go now, get some food yourself and then go to your bed. You look ready to drop."

"And - am I to be punished?" The words came almost by themselves.

"No. I can ill-afford to lose either an expensive horse or an expensive slave, and I am pleased to have you both returned."

And that was all. Caradoc was too tired to think straight, to feel gratitude or resentment or grief at the chance he had missed. Too tired to do anything at all but gulp down a plate of food and throw himself exhausted on his bed.

By morning, the events of the last two days seemed almost like a dream. Caradoc returned to his duties with Dominus and the other horses and apart from a few sniggers and knowing looks from the other slaves, everything seemed as before. Cassius, however, would not let the matter alone, as he found when they cleaned the horses' stalls together that morning.

"I thought we'd seen the last of you, and good riddance! But no, back you come, and manage to worm your way into the master's good graces again! Well, I've never liked you and I like you even less as time goes by. As a matter of fact, it was me who flicked that whip at the horse and made him bolt! I only meant you to take a tumble, mind, not go haring off. I couldn't believe you were stupid enough to come back like that. I wouldn't have! But then you've always been a bit of a simpleton, haven't you, barbarian?"

However hard Caradoc tried to ignore the needling of Cassius, sooner or later it always seemed to get under his skin. He'd like to fetch him a good clout for flicking that whip! But he resisted the urge, and pitched the last forkful of dung into the barrow. When he wheeled it away, Cassius followed, walking annoyingly close beside him.

"What was it like, being free again? How far did you get? Were you scared? Is that why you came back?"

Caradoc didn't answer. Seeing that he was getting no response to his questioning, Cassius's mood changed swiftly and maliciously.

"Don't talk then, barbarian! Really think you're somebody, don't you? Well, you're less than that dung in the barrow, really! I owe you one, too, for making me look a fool in front of the master and his friend. I promised I'd pay you back and I will, too, the first chance I get!"

Caradoc bore all this in silence. He was just too tired to have another fight, and it wasn't worth it anyway. Cassius was annoying and he was spiteful, but his words and threats were only a lot of hot air.

Or so he thought. Later that same day, though, he was to change his mind. When the exercising and evening work were done, Caradoc returned to his room in the slave quarters to find the older boy there, with an expression of glee upon his sharp face. Caradoc's wooden chest was open and his few possessions scattered over the floor. Cassius had obviously been rummaging through it.

"What are you doing with my things?"

"Looking," said Cassius gloatingly. "And I found something too, among those evil-smelling skins you call clothes. Something interesting. Very interesting."

He pushed his face up close to Caradoc's with a sneer. "Think you're somebody, don't you, barbarian? Chief's son, crack horseman, hob-nobbing with the master and the lady? Think you can get away with murder, don't you? Well, I've found something that will soon change their opinions."

"What do you mean?"

"I mean you're a thief, after all, that's what I mean! You might not have got away with stealing the horse, but I've found something else you've been thieving from our Roman masters. I've got the evidence right here, to prove it. I wonder what they'll think of this?"

He held up between finger and thumb a ring of dull gold, such as most of the Romans wore.

"Found this in your pouch, I did! You can't deny it, can you? And I'm off to our master to see what he has to say about it!"

Chapter 19

"Caradoc, is this true?"

Standing before the keen searching eyes of Justus Pollus, Caradoc squared his shoulders. "I am not a thief."

"Yet this ring was in your possession, was it not?"

"Yes."

"It is a Roman ring." Justus had the ring in his fingers, turning it thoughtfully this way and that.

"Yes."

"Explain then - if you can."

"It was given to me by a Roman soldier."

Justus looked as though he found this statement difficult to believe.

"And in what circumstances, pray?"

Caradoc began to sweat a little in the unaccustomed warmth. They were in the atrium, where, in spite of the chill outdoors, the exotic plants bloomed and flowered, cosseted by the warm air flowing up from beneath the marbled floors.

"Last spring, my father took a Roman soldier

prisoner after a battle. The Druids intended to sacrifice him on May Day, and we had him in the village until - "

Caradoc's story was suddenly interrupted. The lady Helena had been sitting sewing in a far corner of the atrium, behind the splashing fountain, staying out of the conversation which was really her husband's affair, but at the same time keeping a watchful eye on the proceedings. Now she dropped her needlework and rose to her feet.

"Justus, let me see that ring!"

Justus turned his head in mild annoyance, "My dear, please do not interfere. I believe I have the measure of this boy, and I will get the truth of this, have no fear. I know you are interested in him because he professes your faith, but pray allow me to - "

He broke off, for his wife had taken the ring from his fingers and was examining it closely, peering at the inside rim. "It is! It's his ring - I bought it myself for him, and there are the words I had inscribed! Justus - this ring belongs to our son - to Lucius!"

She turned to Caradoc. "So you are that brave boy! The one our son told us of, who risked his own life to cut his bonds and set him free! Oh Justus, don't you see? Caradoc is the one to whom Lucius owes his life!"

The retired Roman soldier and his slave stared at each other in mutual astonishment as the truth slowly dawned on each of them. Helena embraced her husband and then Caradoc, laughing at their expressions.

She said "To think that all these weeks we never guessed! I have long wished to be able to thank the brave lad who saved the life of our son! I always knew you to be a boy of integrity, but who would have thought - "

she clasped her hands together in wordless delight.

Justus Pollus sat down rather heavily in his chair. The revelations of the last few moments had been something of a shock to him, and he needed time to adjust. He said at last, rather gruffly, "You have our heartfelt thanks for what you did for our son, and you shall be rewarded."

His wife, who had been pacing about the atrium in her excitement, whirled suddenly to face him. "Justus! I have a thought! You have spoken truly that this boy should be rewarded - and what better reward than granting him his freedom? It is what he wants more than anything. And he richly deserves it. Not only did he bring back your rebellious horse, but unknown to us he also gave us back our only son!"

She turned to Caradoc and went on, "Lucius is back in Rome with his legion at present. But last August he was married to the daughter of two of our closest friends, a sweet and beautiful maiden. By another summer, God willing, we shall all be the proudest of grandparents - " she faced her husband again. "Think of all we would have lost if those wicked pagan priests had had their way, my husband! Are not the lives of our son and future grandchildren of more worth than the twenty-one sestertiums you paid for that boy?"

Caradoc looked from her pleading face to the keen, shrewd weather-beaten one of her husband, hardly daring to hope. The Roman cleared his throat. "Yes. You are right. You shall go free, Caradoc, and return to your people."

Caradoc felt a huge lump rise in his throat and his eyes swam with tears. He tried to stammer out his thanks. Justus Pollus appeared deep in thought, his chin in his hands. Then he lifted his head, and Caradoc was sure that he saw a twinkle in the keen dark eye. "Never let it be said that I am becoming tight-fisted in my old age! I must remember that human life - or horseflesh for that matter - cannot always be measured in terms of money! To prove I am in earnest, you shall take the horse Dominus with you when you leave to join your people." He cleared his throat again, warming to his theme. "Also, as the journey is long and hazardous, you shall take with you another slave - of your choosing - also mounted and equipped."

Caradoc felt his jaw drop, and heard the lady give a gasp of amazement. He tried to speak again, but Helena was beside him, gently hurrying him out of the atrium. "Go quickly, and make your preparations, before he changes his mind! Though I don't think he will - he is a man of his word. But it's quite unknown for him to give away slaves and horses, as though they cost nothing! Who would have thought I'd live to see the day - "

Caradoc heard her laugh softly as she closed the door behind him. He walked back to the slave quarters with his head in a whirl. Events had taken place at such a speed that he felt overwhelmed. Near the stable yard Cassius was slyly looking out for him.

"Finished with you, have they?"

"Yes."

"Found you guilty?"

"No."

"Don't give me that! I know very well you're a thief and so do they! I can tell by the look on your face. What's your punishment to be, then? A scourging? Twenty lashes? Or a hanging by your thumbs to make you consider the error of your ways?"

"No," said Caradoc. "As a matter of fact, they're setting me free."

He saw the face of Cassius collapse into a look of baffled defeat, and suddenly all the resentment and animosity he had felt for the other boy was drowned in a wave of pity. Out of the relief and elation that filled him, he heard himself say "I am allowed to take with me another slave, who will be free too. Do you want to come with me?"

He looked down at the cobblestones of the yard. There was a gasp followed by a stunned silence. Caradoc raised his head to see that Cassius was standing with staring eyes and all the colour drained from his face.

"You're joking!"

"No, I mean it. You've always wanted to be free. Here's your chance. You're a good horseman and you'd soon learn the ways of our tribe - "

Still deathly white, Cassius slowly shook his head, his voice hardly more than a whisper. "No."

"But - you'd be free! We can forget all this stupid quarrelling - we'd both be free - "

But the older boy would not raise his head. "No, I can't. I couldn't. You don't understand - " He turned and stumbled away, not looking at Caradoc.

Caradoc stared after him in wonder and pity and dawning understanding. Though Cassius, knowing nothing but slavery, had longed all his life for freedom, the fear of the unknown was too great for him to take the chance when it was offered.

Sadly, he was not alone. Not a slave was to be found

129

at the farm of Justus Pollus who would venture into the wild borderlands with Caradoc. In the event, it was the Roman himself, his wrist newly out of its dressings, who accompanied the boy on the first part of his journey. They had bidden the lady Helena an affectionate farewell and, wrapped in warm cloaks, left behind the Roman villa on the outskirts of Glevum, riding all day and spending the first night at the villa of a friend. At first light next morning they were off again, heading for the distant hills of the Welsh border.

"I shall be sorry to let you go," said the old soldier, as they set out at a brisk canter along a stretch of straight hard road. "You are as fine a horseman as any boy I have seen - better than Lucius was at the same age. It was always the glory of war and battle he was after, from when he was a little fellow, though I daresay I am to blame for that as much as anyone."

Caradoc smiled. "My brother is just the same." Then he sobered, remembering that he had no guarantee that Owain still lived.

"And what about you?" asked Justus, seeing the sober look. "I think you are a little different, are you not?"

Caradoc was silent for a moment, feeling the powerful muscular body of the horse under him and listening to the clop of well-shod hooves on the hard surface. Then he said, "I don't see much glory in bloodshed and battle, except when we have to defend ourselves. I have always wanted to have time to find out about things, to read and study, to figure out better ways of living - " He stammered to a halt, not quite knowing how to explain himself.

"Ah - a scholar and a thinker!" said Justus with a smile. "Well, the world has need of all sorts, I have no doubt. I am just a simple soldier turned farmer, myself. But I too have no liking for the way our civilized world seems to be heading, and especially the excesses of Rome and of our Emperor. Sometimes I fear for the future of our Empire and wonder if it can last. My wife, now, insists that it is the Christians who in the end will see victory. Do you agree? And how will it happen?"

"We are taught that one day the Lord Christ will come again to set up his Kingdom and rule all the earth," said Caradoc slowly, a little out of his depth at having his opinions asked. "But I don't know how it will happen, or what will go before. These are things hard to understand."

Justus grunted in agreement. "And yet there is an inner peace about the followers of the Lord Christ. I have seen it even among those who died in the arena, and wondered at it. One day I may even decide to follow him myself, who knows?"

Justus and Caradoc parted company before they left the low-lying farming country, Justus saying that it was a long cold ride home for his stiff old bones. Caradoc was sorry to see him go. It was still a long and lonely distance to his home, and away from the good Roman roads the way would be slow and rough, in spite of the sturdy horse under him.

Boy and horse were both tired, and Caradoc's limbs were stiff with cold by the time darkness began to fall again. Before them the snow-capped mountain peaks jutted from the wooded slopes, still a day's ride away. He must find shelter for the night for himself and the horse.

Almost without thinking, he had guided the horse's head in the direction of the house of monks, and in the late afternoon the group of buildings, huddled close to the bare earth, came into sight by the light of a thin moon.

Chapter 20

It was almost like that first time at the monks' house, seeming now so long ago, except that this time he rode a fine stallion instead of being trussed like a pheasant on the back of a small donkey. Again the door was flung wide, and the dark bulk of a man in monks garb appeared against the dim light, holding high a lighted torch. Caradoc saw with joy that it was Brother John.

The monk did not at first recognise him. "What can I do for you, young master? It is late to be abroad."

"Brother John, don't you know me?"

Caradoc flung a leg over the side of the horse and dropped stiffly to the ground, aching in every joint. Holding the reins, he moved closer so that the torchlight fell on his face.

"Caradoc?" The old man's voice sounded doubtful at first, changing to delighted recognition and amazement. "Caradoc! It is you! After all this time - alive! God be praised!"

There was a sudden gentle murmur of mens' voices, as others came hurrying to see, peering into the circle of torchlight, astonished and overjoyed at the sight of the boy, exclaiming at his height and growth and the magnificent horse standing with drooping head behind him. They were all there - John and Alwyn, Dafyd and Idris and the rest. Even the same old donkey was there, judging by the irritated braying that came suddenly from the stable.

Caradoc laughed aloud, his heart strangely moved by the old familiar faces. "Yes, it is I. Will you take me in for the night? And have you somewhere that my horse might be sheltered?"

A temporary stall was found for Dominus, next to the outraged donkey, who retreated in silent resentment to the very far end of the building. Dafyd, his garment tucked up, brought water and fodder while Caradoc rubbed down and bedded the horse with barley straw.

"A magnificent animal, indeed," the monk remarked, placing the good hay in the manger. "Yours?"

"Mine," said Caradoc, with a caress to the shining black flank. "I'll tell you all about him, and everything else, when I've finished here."

The Monks sat up long after their usual time for retiring for the night, listening in wonder to the tale the boy told as he hungrily ate his supper.

"We remember well the day the invaders came," said John at last, his face thoughtful in the flickering torchlight. "We watched them march in their proud ranks up the valley and into the woods. We knew it was your village they attacked. We even heard, faintly, the clashing and shouting of battle when they reached it." He paused, looking into the boy's face. "And we watched them march away, with shouts of victory, never knowing that they took you with them as prisoner."

Caradoc held his breath, hardly daring to mention the thing that was closest to his heart. "Brother John - do you - have you heard or seen anything of my people since that day?"

The monk shook his head slowly, deep compassion in his eyes. He put out a hand to touch the boy's shoulder. "I am sorry, my son. I can see that you hoped to find some of your people alive still. But you must prepare yourself to face the sad truth. I am afraid no-one was left alive - or at any rate, none survived long that dreadful battle."

Caradoc's heart sank with a frightening lurch. He shook off the comforting hand. "How do you know?"

The old man spoke gently. "Thinking of you, I made it my business to investigate. Some time later, I took the old donkey and travelled up to where your hunting runs used to be. In the past, if I had happened to be in the woods searching for some strayed animal, or gathering berries, I had sometimes seen your parties of men, or groups of young boys, passing there with their spears and bows and hunting dogs. I always took care to keep out of sight, of course. Since the battle, no-one has gone to the hunt. Now the runs are tangled and overgrown with disuse. Later on, in midsummer when the days are long and light, I ventured up as far as the belt of trees surrounding your earthworks. I found no sign of life, only a couple of horses's carcases, unburied and rotting, with blow-flies and carrion crows thick about them. There was a stink of death all about the place. I am sorry, my son."

Caradoc put head in his hands in an agony of pain.

There was nothing left to come home to, after all. He had
half-expected this, but all the time he had somehow kept
alive a faint gleam of hope. Now, with the gentle
compassionate words of the monk, all hope was gone.

Brother John reached out and touched him gently. "I
am sorry, my son" he repeated. "This is sad news for
your homecoming. I can see that you had returned with
hopes that I have dashed. We share your grief, for we
are one in Christ. May He help you to bear it."

Caradoc raised his head to the figure of the suffering
Christ on the wall, and felt the hot tears trickle down his
cheeks.

Yet he found there was somehow a comfort to be
found in the quiet routine of the monks' life. All of them
welcomed Caradoc, assuring him that he could make his
home with them, taking up his work and study where he
had left off. In just the space of a week or two the gentle
rhythm of outside jobs and indoor work, of prayer and
meditation and study began to bring an easement to the
raw grief in his heart. He helped Alwyn to make the
roofs secure against the coming winter, cut wood and
built an extension to the stable to house Dominus,
exercised the horse, chopped vegetables and scrubbed
pots. And when the work was done, there was the
comfort of books and parchments, which in themselves
brought a kind of healing. The first bitter pain of loss and
loneliness began to ease.

Winter was really here, and there came a day when
a bitter North wind moaned about the low buildings and
rattled the bare branches of the hazels. Brother Alwyn
forecast a fall of sleet or even snow within the next few
days, the first for the lower lands, though the mountain

tops had been white for weeks.

Caradoc went to bed with a restlessness in his heart. Up in the woods the forest trees would be swaying and tossing their branches, the last clinging autumn leaves sent spinning from the twigs to whirl and dance under the trees and finally pile in drifts along the banks and under the tree roots. He had a sudden longing to be there, among the trees, to see his own village again even if it held no life. The longing grew as he tossed and turned restlessly, listening to the wind moaning and whistling under the eaves. In the morning he was up early, and as it grew light stood at the door with his face turned in the direction of his old home, watching dawn break over the wind-tossed forest slopes.

"What troubles you, my son?"

He jumped. He hadn't noticed that Brother John had joined him at the door, his hood over his head against the bitter wind.

"I was thinking - " he began, and hesitated, because he couldn't really put into words what his thoughts had been. Then he said suddenly, "I was thinking that I will ride up to my village just once more. Today. I can get back before dark if I hurry, on Dominus."

The monk looked grave. "Is that wise? Would it not be distressing? You know not what you might find there. And I doubt that you would get there and back before nightfall, these short dark days. And the wind is still rising."

Caradoc tried to explain that it was the wind and stormy weather that had made him homesick for one more sight of his village, no matter what he might find. He said, "If I don't go now the snow will come and I won't be able to for months. Dominus travels swiftly, and if night catches up with us he and I can find shelter somewhere together. I must go, just this once more."

Brother John did not try to dissuade him further. After breakfast, with no more delay, Caradoc wrapped himself in his warm cloak, mounted the black horse and galloped away towards the wooded slopes with the fierce wind in his face.

It was a cold ride, with the wind against him all the way, whipping at his cloak and filling his eyes with stinging tears. He soon saw that the short winter day would indeed not be long enough to get to the village and back. In fact, dusk was already beginning to fall when at last he reached the edge of the forest. His heart began to race as they entered the trees, hearing the bare branches creak and toss and sway all about him. But at least the trees broke the bitter chill of the wind as they began to climb.

Caradoc strained his eyes ahead to get the first glimpse of the looming earthworks, but by now it was almost dark and the air was full of the uneasy sound of trees tossed and harried by the wind. It was light enough though to see the gleam of bones among the brown undergrowth - a horse's skeleton, and, a little further on, another - picked clean now and partly covered by fallen leaves. He dug his heels into the flank of Dominus and pressed on, reaching at last the mouth of the pass and steering the horse's head into it.

The village lay deathly silent, no sentinel at his post, no children at play, the windswept ground bare between the huts and the huts themselves falling into disrepair. Caradoc's eyes darted to right and left, but there was no sign of life to be seen, not even a dog. Yet, as he rode in between the ramparts, from somewhere there came the bleat of a goat. Next moment a dull glow showed beyond the huts, and he saw that within the circle of sacred stones, blown by the wind and casting weird flickering shadows across the ground, the bonfire still burned.

Chapter 21

The hoofbeats of the horse thudded dully on the bare packed earth as Caradoc rode into the village. He looked around him with eyes blurred with sudden tears at the familiar homes - Morgan's and Madoc's, and over there, the largest and most important hut in the village, the chieftain's hut, his own home. He was puzzled by the fire that still burned. Could some of the Druids be alive still after all these months?

As he dismounted, the goat bleated again, and from the corner of his eye he saw a movement in one of the doorways. Next moment, a small child had appeared, taking a few steps towards him before standing to gaze wonderingly with its thumb in its mouth. Then it was grabbed from behind by its mother, who took one fearful look at horse and rider standing in the twilight, and tried to hide herself and the child inside. He recognised them both, greeting them by name with disbelief and joy.

"Griff! Megan! You are here! It is I, Caradoc!"

All in the space of a few moments, other figures slipped from shadowy doorways to surround him. Small children, mothers with babies, old Rhys and crippled Morgan. So many of his people, thin, haggard, some sick - but alive! They seemed as amazed to see him as he was to see them, surrounding him like a flock of chattering magpies, exclaiming, touching, questioning, staring in wonderment at the tall black horse standing quietly at his shoulder. Caradoc, overwhelmed by the wonder of finding them alive and by their welcome, stretched out his hands and arms to all he could reach, answering their babbled questions as best he could, picking up and holding a small child toddling dangerously close to the hooves of Dominus. Yet all the time his eyes searched eagerly for other faces.

At last a dark shadow appeared from the doorway of the chieftain's hut, roused by the noise.

"Owain!"

Caradoc saw his brother at once, set the small child on its feet, handed the horse's reins to Rhys and sprang forward in greeting. But he stopped in his tracks before he reached the doorway, for even in the dim light he could see that his brother was sadly changed. His face was thin and strained, marred by a terrible scar from forehead to chin on one side, his sturdy figure now stooped and thin, and one of his tunic sleeves hanging empty. Caradoc felt that his brother seemed suddenly smaller, diminished in every way, even physical size - though this may have been because he himself had grown and filled out over the past months. His heart filled with love and pity, and he reached out to put his arms around his brother, something he had not done since they were small children. Owain held himself stiffly at this show of womanly weakness, his mouth twisting in a wry smile.

"So! Once again you are returned from the dead, little brother! We had thought truly never to see you again, this time! And looking well-fed and prosperous too, I see!"

His tone was slightly mocking, as he took in the thick, warmly-lined cloak that Caradoc wore, his warm leggings and boots, and the magnificent horse beside him. Caradoc began to say that he was starving with hunger, but suddenly saw that his brother's face and those of the others was pinched and thin, as though they themselves had not eaten for a long time and were truly near starving. He hesitated, hardly daring to ask, and then said "What of Islean?"

"Inside. She sleeps early these short days. She is feeling the cold, as are many of the old ones. Several have died." He paused and went on, again in a mocking tone "I am afraid you will find things sadly changed. Almost all our men - " he broke off, suddenly unable to continue.

Caradoc had already noticed that very few of the men were present among the women, children and old people. Only Bryn, with an empty eye socket on the left side, Tavis, who limped leaning heavily on a stout staff and Ivor, who seemed not quite aware of his surroundings.

"All that is left of our warriors," said Owain bitterly. "Not much, are they, to come home to? Just as I am not much of a chief, with my sword-arm gone and no more than the strength of a child. We have no able-bodied men here to defend us or hunt food. Even our neighbours think we are not worth bothering with and leave us alone. The Roman dogs might just as well have finished us off with a quick and merciful end."

Caradoc was dismayed by the bitterness in his brother's voice. He said, "I am back now - I and my good strong horse. Between us we can hunt and get food, and do a man's work and more. We will get through, you and I."

Owain gave a short derisive laugh. "We shall see." Caradoc followed him into the chief's hut, where a light burned. Islean woke as they came in and looked up in joyful wonder from a thin, pinched face.

"Caradoc! I was just dreaming that I heard your voice speaking to me, and when I awake, here you are! May God be praised! I will get you food."

Caradoc protested, but his grandmother insisted upon rising and making supper for him from their meagre supplies. He could not help but notice that she too was much frailer and weaker than he remembered.

"It is but poor fare," she apologised, putting a thin stew and coarse bread before him. "Our food must be rationed if it is to last the winter."

"There are plenty of deer in the forest," said Caradoc. "I will try to shoot one tomorrow."

He ate thankfully, telling between mouthfuls of all that had happened since his capture. Outside, the wind was still rising, rattling the bare branches of the trees and blowing smoke from the bonfire in all directions. A thought struck Caradoc suddenly. "The Druids! I have seen nothing of them."

Islean shook her head, sitting close beside Caradoc as though she was afraid he might suddenly disappear again.

"The Druids are no more. The Romans left us to

ourselves, in the end, but before that they killed the Druids, every one."

Owain gave another short laugh. "They took the priests to the highest crags they could find and threw them off. Called it wiping out a nest of hornets."

He walked to the door and peered out into the wind.

"How it blows! I must make sure that the stock pens are secure. And I'll stable that fine black horse of yours, too." He left the room, his empty sleeve flapping.

Islean gazed sadly after him. "He is much changed, your brother. Hurt in mind and spirit as well as in body, I fear. He was wounded almost unto death, and is only slowly recovering his strength."

She sighed. Another gust of wind shook the building, and smoke from the bonfire drifted in through the doorway. Caradoc got up and closed it after his brother. He was thoughtful for a moment. Then he said "Islean, if the Druids are dead, how is it that the sacred fire still burns?"

Islean nodded tiredly. "The women keep it going. They are afraid of what might happen if they let it go out. I have tried to talk to them of the Lord Christ, and I know that many are longing in their hearts to follow him. But a fear lingers about this place. The Druids are gone, but their influence remains."

Caradoc was silent for a moment, staring at their own small fire. Then he said, "Islean, you and I both believe in the Lord Christ. The Scriptures say that if any two of his followers agree on anything they ask Him, it shall be done for them by their Father in Heaven. It is written that the followers of Christ have His power, by the Holy Spirit, to do the works he did, to heal and to cast out evil, to bind and to loose. You and I, agreeing together, can bind the powers of darkness left by the Druids here."

Islean gazed at him with awe in her tired old eyes, and a touch of wistfulness. "How I wish I could learn the teachings of the Holy Scriptures as you have! I believe what you say! Let us agree together."

So, hands clasped tightly in the flickering firelight, Caradoc and his grandmother, in the name of Jesus Christ, bound the powers of darkness and evil that had held so tightly the people of the village.

During the night the wind increased to a gale, roaring through the tall trees, taking twigs and branches and tossing them as though they were no more than wisps of dry grass. Rain and sleet lashed down on the thatched roofs of the huts huddled close against the mountainside. There were ominous cracks and crashes from the surrounding forest as trees were torn up by their roots, and people woke and listened, wondering fearfully at the savagery of the storm. In the chieftain's hut, Caradoc slept soundly until just after midnight, when he was awakened by an enormous crash close by.

Chapter 22

The first of the tall oaks had come crashing to the ground with a mighty rending and tearing up of roots sunk deep into the soil for generations. Caradoc was immediately on his feet, leaping from his old couch of boughs and animal skins, pulling on his outer garments and running for the doorway. He was met by tearing winds that snatched his breath, and lashing rain which soaked him through in seconds. Against the dark sky showed the darker shape of the trees, tossing their branches in tortured, frenzied movements about the huddle of thatched huts.

Staggering across the clearing with the rain and wind full in his face, Caradoc found that the fallen tree had reached right across the clearing, landing with its topmost branches partly across the roof of one of the huts penetrating the thatch. A low sobbing and the wail of a child sounded from within.

Pushing past the massive trunk with its spreading branches and bare twigs that scratched his face, Caradoc found the door and pushed it open. As he entered he was aware that someone else followed him close behind. Owain too had been awakened by the downfall of the giant oak and was close on his heels.

The hut belonged to the woman Megan and her children. "Megan! Megan!" called Owain urgently in the darkness, "where are you? Where are the children?"

A shaky answer came from one corner. "We are here. The children are safe, but I am pinned by branches."

It was difficult work to release the trapped woman in pitch darkness, with the rain lashing in through the holes in the roof and terrified small children sobbing and trying to cling to their knees, but between them the two brothers lifted the bough that had fallen across her legs. She scrambled to her feet, scratched and bruised but with no bones broken, and between them they gathered together the frightened children. With surprising gentleness Owain steered Megan out of the doorway, the youngest child in his good arm.

"Come, I'll take all of you to my own hut. You must get the children's wet clothes off and wrap them in dry covers."

Following them from the wrecked hut, Caradoc became aware of a stamping of hooves and a frightened neighing from the stables. Battling his way across, he found Dominus snorting with fright in his stall, plunging and trying to rear against the halter by which he was tied. Speaking calmly, the boy made his way in the darkness to the horse's head, risking a kick from the mighty restless hooves.

"Dominus, Dominus - quiet now, quiet! It is I, there is nothing to fear! Just wind and rain, and a falling tree.

Quietly now, quiet!"

The horse's panic gradually died, and he quietened to the soothing voice and touch of the boy. From the adjoining stalls came the voice of Owain, who had returned and was calming the other frightened horses. In a few minutes he had appeared suddenly at the doorway of the black stallion's stall, a blacker shape against the darkness.

"They are quieter now, and no other buildings are damaged. I think the storm is dying a little." He paused and went on in his old half-sneering way "You speak the enemy tongue as one born to it, little brother. Is that not a little disloyal now that you are back with your own people?"

Caradoc was still rubbing the neck of the black stallion and talking soothingly into his ear. He said, "I find it easy to learn other tongues, especially when my own is not spoken. I have heard only English and the Roman tongue for many weeks. I speak the Roman to the horse because it is what he understands best. It is not disloyalty."

Both of them were silent for a moment, listening to the roar of wind in the treetops and the lash of rain. Then Owain said, a little grudgingly, "He is indeed a fine horse."

"He is called Dominus," said Caradoc. "In the Roman tongue that means lordly or masterful. It is a fitting name, I think."

Suddenly a thought came to his mind that seemd to pierce him through as painfully as a spearhead. He struggled against it for a moment, but after a while almost against his will he heard his own voice saying,

"Dominus is a horse who ought to belong to a chieftain. I give him to you, brother. He is yours."

There was silence for a moment. In the darkness Caradoc buried his face against the horse's warm neck, holding his breath. He sensed that a struggle was taking place in his brother's mind and heart in response to his offer. Owain had always had the very best of the tribe's horses, but never one approaching the magnificence of Dominus. With such a mount, even crippled as he was, Owain could surely gain back some of the respect and self-confidence he had lost.

But Owain said at last, a little gruffly, "I thank you, brother, but the horse is yours. You are the one who has mastered him and who speaks his language. He belongs to you, and you deserve him."

He cleared his throat and went on, "I am wet and cold, and am going back to my bed now. I think the storm will blow itself out by the morning."

His dark shape disappeared from the doorway. Caradoc let out his breath in a long sigh. Dominus was still his own. After a while, when the horse folded his legs under him and lay down to rest, Caradoc lay down too, huddled in the dry bracken against the warm black back. When dawn broke over a storm-tossed village they were both sound asleep.

A little later the boy emerged to find that the rain had stopped, the wind died to occasional fierce gusts, and that a thin sun shone from a pale grey rain-washed sky. He looked around on a scene of devastation. Several of the huts had patches of thatch torn away from their roofs, and Megan's hut lay battered, half obscured by the branches of the tall oak. Other branches and boughs littered the clearing, and in the forest many other trees had fallen, lying on the ground with their roots exposed to the air or leaning drunkenly for support against others that still stood.

Above the dwellings, where the ancient stones of the Druids stood, six or seven of the giant oaks in the grove had fallen, lying haphazardly against the stones or across the trunks of others that had fallen also. The sacred fire in the centre had gone out, its ashes grey and dead, damply sifting over the wet ground. As the villagers emerged, shivering and red-eyed, their gaze turned at once to the grove and the stones. They looked at one another in silence, not knowing what to say. Such a thing had never happened before in the living memory of any of them.

Caradoc, at the door of the stable, was struck again with pity at their thinness, their pallor and helplessness. Without Tiernan, and without the Druids and their young warriors, they seemed like a flock of mountain sheep with no-one to shepherd them. But he knew, in a sudden moment of revelation, that the power of the Druids was broken. The fear that had bound their minds and hearts was no longer there.

He felt his own heart lift. He sprang to a fallen trunk and stood on it, smiling down at them. "I greet you all! Are any sick, or injured in the storm?"

There was a murmur of voices and shaking of heads. Megan was brusied and scratched, some had had their beds and posessions soaked as the rain lashed in through gaps and holes, but otherwise all were well.

"Good! Then we'll make fires first of all, and cook breakfast. After that I'll help any who need their homes repaired. Then we'll see about some fresh meat. Will anyone help me hunt?"

Ceri and Huw, boys of ten or eleven, came forward eagerly. "We'll help, Caradoc. We've got our bows and arrows, and spears."

Caradoc smiled. "Good. I'll be glad of some sensible men."

Suddenly he saw from the corner of his eye that Owain had risen and emerged from their own hut. He felt a fresh stab of shock and pity at the sight of his brother in the daylight, thin and pale and stooped like an old man. Owain paused for a moment in the doorway, watching the scene, his expression unfathomable as he took in the sight of his strong, whole brother, the eager children pressing about him, the attitudes of the broken men and women, almost beaten but perhaps this morning with the tiniest seeds of hope newly planted in their hearts.

All were looking at Caradoc, clamouring for instruction and encouragement.

"Caradoc! Caradoc!" said Ceri, waving a spear in his face. "This is my spear, look! I've kept it good and sharp. Test it!"

"Mine, too," said Huw jostling for attention. "Mine is the sharpest. Isn't it, Caradoc?"

Old crippled Morgan stepped forward. "Be off with you, boys! Don't bother him with your nonsense! Caradoc, if you want to spend the day hunting meat, Ivor and Tavis and I can mend the huts. We can manage it between us."

Already the apathy and hopelessness had gone from the eyes of the villagers. Some of the women took their leather buckets and went to fetch clean water from the spring, while others searched for dry kindling to start the cooking fires. A toddler or two ran out of the huts to gaze admiringly at Caradoc.

Over their heads, Caradoc watched as Owain walked slowly towards him, his lips twisted in a half-bitter smile. Gone now was the brave and strong young chieftain leading his people into battle, and in his place stood a maimed and weakened youth, forced to watch in humiliation as his younger brother took the lead. Caradoc's heart twisted again with pity.

Yet he remembered suddenly the generous sense of justice that had caused Owain to refuse Caradoc's offer of the great black horse, which would have done so much to restore his sense of self-esteem. He thought too of the gentleness with which Owain had carried Megan's youngest child during the storm, and calmed and soothed the frightened family. Clearly his brother posessed qualities of leadership still, together with a new touch of gentleness and compassion.

A quarrel had broken out in earnest between the two ten-year-olds, and one of them was bawling from a slight prick from a spearhead, while the other loudly protested his innocence. One of their mothers fetched her child a clout while the other looked appealingly at Caradoc.

"They have grown uncontrolled, lacking fathers. Can you instil some discipline into them?"

The old men were still waiting for instructions, their rheumy eyes upon him.

Suddenly Caradoc knew what he must do. His eyes still upon Owain, he jumped from the log and bounded across to meet his brother. Taking Owain's good hand in his own, he lifted it high into the air.

"Listen, everyone! Here is your chief! He will decide what we are to do! Come to the chieftain's hut after your breakfasts, and he will settle your disputes, answer your questions and instruct you in the affairs of the day. I speak only as his second-in-command. It is to him you must come!"

The people murmured and nodded in agreement. "Aye. He's right. The young chief looks stronger already. He'll be hunting again before long, himself." They began to scatter and go their various ways. Owain and Caradoc together made their way to the chief's hut. Owain spoke for the first time with a note of wryness. "You've put new life in them. And in me. Maybe in time I'll be of some real use again." He lifted his hand in a half-mocking salute, and then let it fall for a moment on Caradoc's shoulder. "I never knew you had it in you, little brother. Everything's changed already."

Caradoc smiled, turning to look again with love at the village beginning to come to life before him. He wanted to tell Owain, and all of them, that it was the power of the Lord Christ, and not his own, that made the difference, that had already begun to work in response to his own prayers and those of Islean. No-one had offered to re-light the sacred fire, or expressed fear at the desecration of the grove. They were free, although they did not yet know it, free to live without the shadow of fear and to accept the teaching of the better way.

One day, soon, he would begin to tell them of the Lord Christ and of his power to change lives. For a moment, he thought of Brother John and the monks in the little community below, knowing that they waited for him to return to their quiet life of worship and study. The thought brought a twinge of regret. Maybe one day he would be free to go back to them

But for now, here was this cold, windswept, battered village full of weak and hungry people, and here was his brother in need of his support in leading them. Entering the hut with Owain, and seeing Islean's face, thin and worn yet this morning newly hopeful, he knew that at least for the time, his place was here among his own people where the wind blew free among the tall oaks.

OTHER BOOKS AVAILABLE FROM
CHRISTIAN FOCUS PUBLICATIONS

OFFSIDE IN ECUATINA

Cliff Rennie

The World Cup is threatened by a power-hungry drug
baron. Danger lurks at every corner, but Doug Mackay,
football star, is determined to thwart the criminals. In
the process he becomes a national hero.

ISBN 1 87167 669 X
£2.50   128pp

THAT FINAL SUMMER

Margaret Smith

Conflict and tension mount during the long hot summer. Graham is involved in poaching, Sheleen discovers she is adopted and Timmy has a serious illness. All the ingredients for a gripping read.

ISBN 1 87167 691 6

£2.95   128pp

THE BROKEN BOW

Pauline Thompson

When Kisoo agrees to meet his brother for a moonlight hunting expedition, he gets into more trouble than he expected. Breaking the stranger's bow and running away, Kisso meets up with people who can tell him about a special friend who can forgive him.

ISBN 1 87167 698 3
£2.95   128pp

THE OUTSIDERS

Margaret Smith

Donna finds herself at logger-heads with Stewart Steele. He's an incomer to the area and she thinks he's stealing from her. But Stewart is not taking the blame, and there's another side to him besides his tough image.

ISBN 1 87167 652 5
£2.50   128pp

TRUE GOLD

Cliff Rennie

The huge Olympic stadium was full of cheering spectators. Among them was Jason anxiously scanning his programme. Gordon's race was due to start in just a few minutes. Surely nothing or no one could stop him going for gold. Then suddenly Jason gasped in horror. Gordon was in deadly danger! But what could he do?

ISBN 1 87167 690 8
£2.95   128pp